Choosing Sides

Karen Meyer

Sable
CREEK
PRESS

Other books authored by Karen Meyer

Conflict at Chillicothe
Battle at Blue Licks
Missing at Marietta
Whispers at Marietta
North to Freedom
The Tiara Mystery
Simon Kenton, Unlikely Hero
From Wimpy to Winning

Visit the author's website ohiofrontierhistorylady.com

Cover and text design by Diane King, dkingdesigner.com

Scripture taken from the King James Version. Public domain.

Published by Sable Creek Press
sablecreekpress.com

Names: Meyer, Karen, 1943- author.
Title: Choosing sides / Karen Meyer.
Description: [Glendale, Arizona] : Sable Creek Press, [2020] | Interest age level: 008-012. | Summary: "In 1875, Gilbert Freeman and the nation were deeply divided over the evils of alcohol, sparking the Temperance Movement. When Gilbert runs away from his Ohio farm, he plans to leave his troubles behind. Instead, he stumbles into the middle of the fierce fight against the opening of a saloon in the town of Westerville"--Provided by publisher.
Identifiers: ISBN 9780578615073
Subjects: LCSH: Runaways--Ohio--Juvenile fiction. | Temperance--Ohio--Juvenile fiction. | Bars (Drinking establishments)--Ohio--Juvenile fiction. | Choice (Psychology)--Juvenile fiction. | CYAC: Runaways--Ohio--Fiction. | Temperance--Ohio--Fiction. | Bars (Drinking establishments)--Ohio--Fiction. | Choice (Psychology)--Fiction. | LCGFT: Historical fiction.
Classification: LCC PZ7.M49 Ch 2020 | DDC [Fic]--dc23

Acknowledgments

Every author needs helpers and encouragers. My heartfelt thanks go to my editor, Christine Kohler, who gave me great advice, making this novel much more polished. Thanks also to my publisher, Janet Shay, who bravely pointed out what needed to change. Thanks to my cover and inside designer, Diane King, for patience in creating another pleasing cover. Thanks to others who encouraged me along the way: my husband who gave opinions on demand, my sister Julie Geist, who didn't want Gilbert to go astray, and my friend, Kathy Davis, who had detailed suggestions on my first draft (always the worst draft.) Thanks for the help of the ladies in Westerville Library's History Center, Nina Thomas and Beth Weinhart. Thank you also to my willing model, grandson Justin Meyer.

Contents

1872 Map of Westerville, Ohio

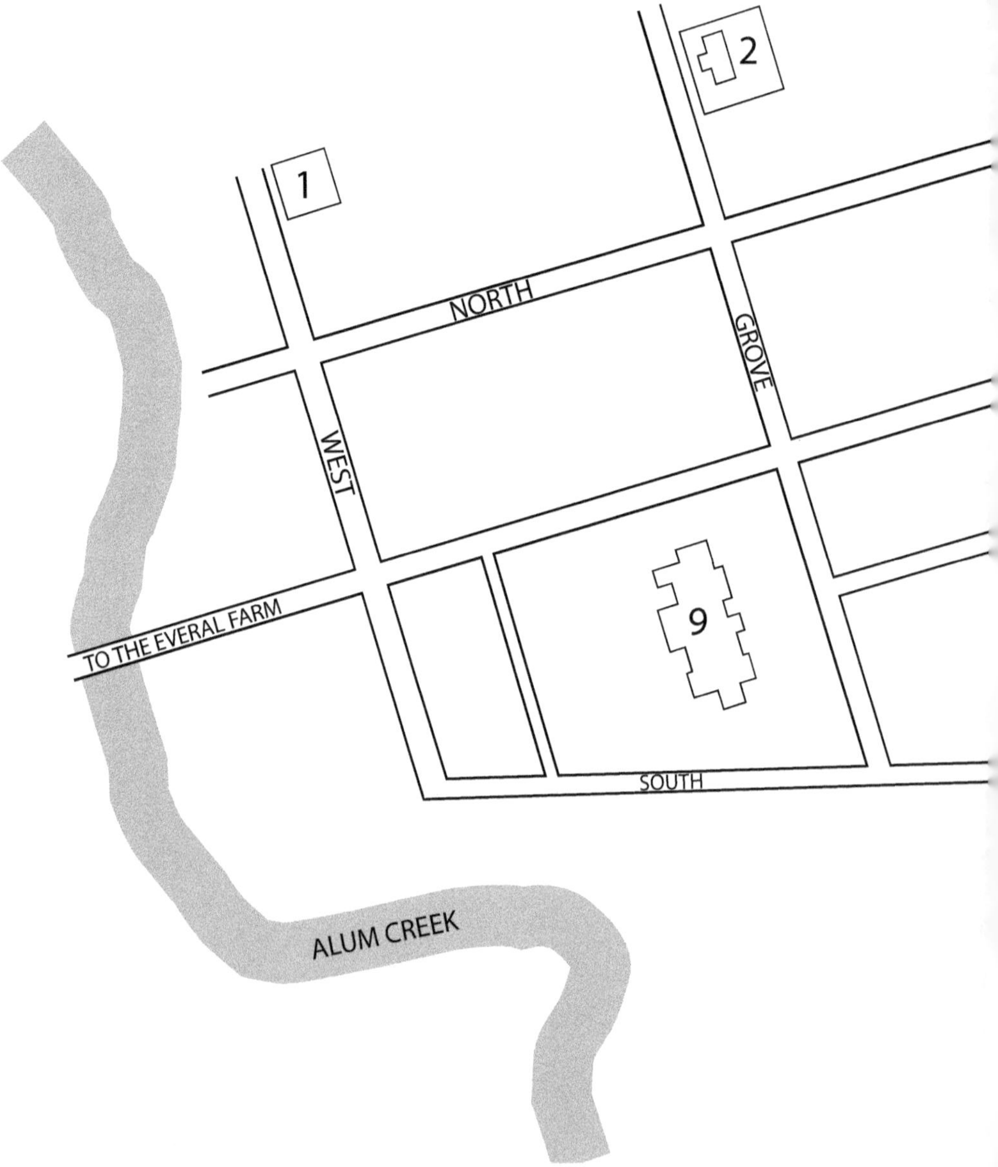

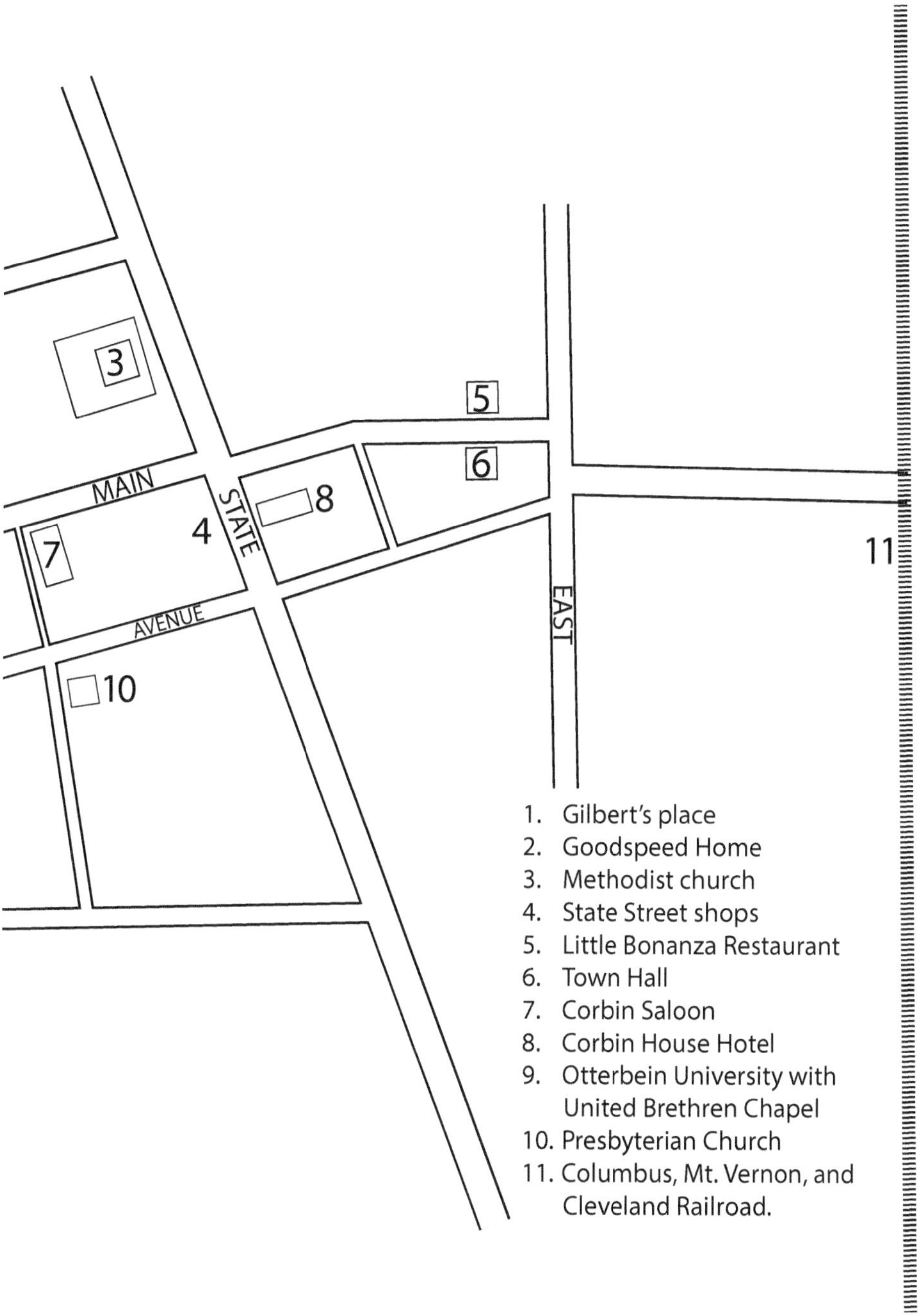

1. Gilbert's place
2. Goodspeed Home
3. Methodist church
4. State Street shops
5. Little Bonanza Restaurant
6. Town Hall
7. Corbin Saloon
8. Corbin House Hotel
9. Otterbein University with United Brethren Chapel
10. Presbyterian Church
11. Columbus, Mt. Vernon, and Cleveland Railroad.

1 Aunt Ruby's Visit

Genoa Township, Ohio
June 15, 1875

Gilbert Freeman gripped the windowsill as a four-wheeled buggy sped toward him past fields showing tiny sprouts of green. Summer would make his struggle with Pa worse.

Behind him his younger sister, Annie, shouted, "Aunt Ruby and Pa will be here any minute! Do something with these." She thrust a stack of newspapers in his direction.

He stashed them behind the kindling box, grabbed the broom, and swept bits of bark under the braided rug. "The kitchen passes my inspection."

Annie put her hands on her hips. "Just look at those muddy footprints from the back door."

Gilbert grimaced. "At least I filled the wood box."

Annie dug into the ragbag in the basement stairs and tossed him a piece of holey underwear. "Here, wet this rag and mop up."

On hands and knees, Gilbert swabbed the smears still left on the floor. "When Aunt Ruby comes, quit bossing me around. You're only eleven, and I'm two whole years older."

Since Ma died of pneumonia, Gilbert felt like a grown man. He gave the floor a last swipe and stuffed the rag behind the umbrella stand.

Annie fluffed the pillows on the divan, straightened the scrolled mirror, and pushed a stray curl out of her eyes.

Pilot's bark brought Gilbert to the living room window in time to see Pa bringing the horses to a halt. "Aunt Ruby's here."

Aunt Ruby Howard was Ma's younger sister. This was only her third visit since Ma died six months ago. She taught school in Mount Vernon, so she couldn't come often. She mended their clothes and fixed meals.

Aunt Ruby burst through the door and opened her arms wide. "How are my favorite niece and nephew?" She hugged Annie and kissed her cheek.

Gilbert hesitated as the generous arms opened for him. His aunt, with her dark eyes and slender figure, looked so much like his mother he felt afresh the pain of missing her.

His aunt held him at arm's length. "I declare, you've grown an inch since I last saw you. But you could use a bit of meat on your bones."

Pa came in and hung up his hat. "Gilbert needs cooking lessons. Meals around here . . . " He trailed off and hurried to carry Ruby's suitcase to the guest room.

Gilbert dared to glance at his sister. Would Pa act grouchy while their aunt visited? Pa sank into one of his moods whenever he had any reminder of Ma. They'd learned to stay out of his way.

Aunt Ruby untied the strings of her bonnet. "Annie, let's you and me rustle up supper tonight. Do I smell a roast cooking?"

Annie smiled and the dimple deepened in her left cheek. "Yes, Gilbert put the pot on the stove hours ago. But we don't know how to make the biscuits. And Gilbert's gravy is awful."

Aunt Ruby hung her bonnet on the hall tree, and they headed to the kitchen. "We'll get to work. After supper, I have the most splendid idea." The two ladies scurried around the kitchen, and Gilbert followed Pa to the barn.

Pa carried the bucket to milk the cows. He glared at Gilbert. "You didn't fix the pasture fence like I told you. I've been gone for two days, and you've let things slide."

Gilbert clenched his fists. "After I milked the cows and fed the animals, I emptied the rest of the hay from the wagon. It looked like rain, and I ran out of time."

"Use your time more wisely. A lazy man always runs short of time."

Gilbert gritted his teeth as he unharnessed the horse and climbed to the hay mow to toss down the hay for the animals. The pitchfork was gone. He looked in the hay wagon and finally found it behind the cow stalls. It took longer than usual to finish his chores, but he didn't feel like hurrying.

He stood in the barn door and scowled at the thunderclouds looming on the horizon. They matched his thoughts. After Ma died, Pa had made him quit school so he could do all the things Ma used to do. But Pa always found fault with everything he did.

Clang, clang. Gilbert dashed from the barn to answer the supper bell. Annie leaned out to warn him. "Pa's mad at you."

"He's always mad at me." As soon as he washed up and slid into his seat, he noticed Pa's sour look.

"You're late. Wasting time again."

Gilbert glanced sideways—Annie and Aunt Ruby looked sympathetic.

Everyone bowed his head. Pa prayed, "Lord, we thank you for a safe journey and for this food we are about to receive. In Jesus' name. Amen."

Gilbert dug in, loading his plate with his aunt's relishes and pickles, and jam for the biscuits. The apple pie set aside for dessert made his mouth water. The only suppers he could fix were meat and potato meals, but he missed all the extras.

The chockfull table reminded him of the funeral supper six months ago, when casseroles and cakes covered the whole table. Each visitor shared a memory of his mother's care during a crisis.

Ma's death was his fault—Gilbert was sure of it—because she'd spent hours in a shivering rain taking care of his calf. That's why she'd caught pneumonia. Pa knew it, too, and that's why he was so mean to Gilbert. If only he'd taken care of the calf himself. If only . . . guilt ate at him something fierce.

Aunt Ruby's voice jerked him back to the present. "Four of us ladies marched to the saloon. It was so cold we were swathed in scarves and heavy coats."

Pa took a bite of biscuit. "Did they let you inside?"

"This time they did not. We'd been inside other saloons, praying and pleading with the owners to quit their liquor sales. We call them pray-ins. But we can pray just as well outside, so we knelt on blankets." Aunt Ruby's musical laugh rang out. "Having praying ladies outside cuts down on the customers. One of the braver patrons took one of our printed pledges to hand to the owner to sign."

Pa shook his head in amazement. "A pledge . . . to quit selling liquor? Did he sign it?"

"No, he refused. But these marches and pray-ins are having an effect all over Ohio. Many of these home-wrecking businesses have closed. Some towns—like Berea, for instance—had fifty women marching. I would've liked to be in that parade."

Gilbert raised his eyebrows as he visualized Aunt Ruby marching against saloons. He admired his aunt's determination. She stood up for her beliefs. He didn't know if he could be as strong as that if he were in such a situation.

Aunt Ruby swirled a bite of roast beef through the gravy before placing it in her mouth. Pa took a bite too, twice as large. Conversation stopped while everyone ate.

Pa reached for a newspaper on the side table. "Did you see the picture in Frank Leslie's Illustrated Newspaper?" He opened it to a page showing a crowd of women in front of a saloon in Logan, Ohio. "Look at them, dressed to the hilt, with fancy hats and muffs. If I owned a saloon, I'd think twice about crossing them."

Gilbert chuckled to himself at the idea of Pa owning a saloon. Pa and Aunt Ruby both had strong views on abstinence—never taking a drop of an intoxicating beverage. Gilbert wasn't sure he agreed with them. His Uncle Bill, Pa's brother, argued that the temperance movement went against the Constitution's guarantee of liberty. Uncle Bill distilled part of his grain into alcohol, said it was easier to get it to market. And Gilbert had seen him drink beer, too.

Aunt Ruby wiped her mouth with her napkin as if to set aside one topic so she could go on with the next. "I have a grand idea for the summer. One you'll all like." She looked around to make sure everyone was listening. "Annie, would you like to spend the next few months at my house? You'd be a big help. And you could learn new household skills."

Annie sprang from her chair and hugged her aunt. "Oh, could I? You could teach me how to make piecrust. I'm terrible at that. And gravy like Ma used to make."

Gilbert and his father finished their meal, ignoring Aunt Ruby's offer. Neither one wanted Annie to disappear for the summer. Annie's sparkle kept their family from spending gloomy evenings staring at the floor. Without Annie, Gilbert knew he'd be stuck dealing with Pa's foul moods by himself. Gilbert searched for a reason Annie should not go live with Aunt Ruby for the summer and he couldn't think of a single one.

"Then it's settled." Aunt Ruby winked at Annie.

Gilbert's heart sank at the idea of being alone with Pa. Pa used to read aloud interesting newspaper articles and tease Gilbert about his cowlick. But since Ma died, he hadn't told a single joke. Gilbert could leave home, too. He was old enough to get a job and fend for himself. Pa could do without him.

2 Gilbert's Big Decision

Aunt Ruby and Annie had been gone for three days. Time dragged on for Gilbert as slowly as an inchworm crawling along a stick. The two rainy days were especially dismal, and he worked at his chores as though he plodded through molasses.

"Gilbert!" Pa's voice cut through his wandering thoughts. "I don't care if it's storming—the animals still need to be fed. A little rain is no excuse for you to be lazy."

"I'm heading to the barn right now." After he'd mucked out the stalls, Gilbert decided to practice what he'd say to convince Pa about his idea for the summer. He perched Pilot on a hay bale—he knew his shaggy brown-and-white dog would listen without interrupting.

"Pa, I'd like to be on my own, get a job this summer and go to school in the fall." Pilot's tail thumped against the straw, and he approved the idea with a doggy smile.

"What?" Pa's angry voice rose from the cow's stall behind Gilbert.

Gilbert jumped. "Pa!"

"What hare-brained idea are you spouting?"

Gilbert gulped. "I want to get a job and go to school."

"You already have a job, right here."

Gilbert's voice quivered. "But Pa, Annie's allowed to go somewhere."

"Well, you're staying here. And forget about going to school, too."

Gilbert balled his fists. "I'm going to school. Whether you like it or not."

"I don't like it." Pa took a step toward him. "As long as you live under my roof, you'll do what I say. And that's final."

"It's not fair!"

"What's unfair? Working for the food you eat and the roof over your head?" Pa threw his hat to the floor. "You're just no count."

Gilbert darted out of the barn into the darkness, keeping a torrent of angry words corked inside. Pa called his name, but Gilbert kept running. With Pilot beside him, he raced down the hill and past the pond, waking a pair of sleeping mallards.

He plunged into the evergreens. The piney scent and springy needles underfoot eased the pressure in his chest, so he slowed to a walk. The dim light outlined a familiar shape along the path ahead—his thinking log. He came there often with Pilot for comfort or to think through decisions. With a sigh, he perched on the log. Pilot settled his muzzle on his master's lap.

"What should I do?" Gilbert let the night sounds soothe him as he stroked Pilot's head. A bullfrog croaked from the pond. "Pa says I'm lazy. He blames me for Ma's death."

A distant chanting rose above the chorus from the crickets and spring peepers. A human voice sang—but it was not Pa—and Gilbert caught a few words. "Lift your goblets boys . . . mirth and wine and song . . . " Gilbert looked toward the road—a light flickered through the woods as if someone carried a lantern.

Curiosity drew Gilbert through the pines to see the singer. It sounded like Old Herman, a farmer from down the road. Gilbert sniffed the air—a cigar. Old Herman, for sure.

Gilbert recalled last year when Old Herman had come home from a drinking spree one night, making a big commotion. The next morning, his wife piled clothes and kitchen things in a wagon and drove off with their three children. The oldest boy, his friend Stanley, waved as the wagon passed. Gilbert missed going fishing for bass in Alum Creek with him.

The lantern swung back and forth, keeping time to the words pouring out at full volume.

Gilbert threaded through the trees and spotted Old Herman, his hat askew, weaving from side to side. He stopped and raised the lantern as Gilbert stepped into sight. "Well . . . hello . . . it's . . . Gilbert."

Gilbert nodded. "You surprised me with your singing."

Herman straightened his hat. "Left early. From a party. Otis and me had . . . a grand time. Till he fell . . . in a stock tank. Ha, ha, ha! He sputtered and splashed."

"Is he all right?"

"Maybe broke his arm. Ha!"

Gilbert frowned. "Nothing funny about a broken arm."

Herman peered into Gilbert's eyes. "Laugh, boy, or you'll cry." He put his arm around his young neighbor, and Gilbert smelled the alcohol fumes on his breath. "Tell me . . . what makes you . . . such a . . . sour-puss?"

Gilbert pulled back. "I had an argument with Pa."

"'Bout what? You're near a man . . . think for yourself."

"Pa won't let me leave. He made me quit school. All he cares about is keeping me here to work like a slave."

Herman's belly laugh echoed back from the trees. "Go! You deserve it. Me . . . I do chores myself. All the . . . time."

Gilbert shook his head. "Pa would tan my hide if I left."

"Go. If your pa . . . needs help. Old Herman . . . close by. Tell him . . . call on me." Herman stuck out his hand. "Shake . . . " Herman lumbered down the road like a bear and disappeared into the darkness.

Gilbert and Pilot picked their way back through the pines. Old Herman was right—Gilbert deserved to be treated like a man if he was doing a man's job. He'd leave tonight.

On his march back home, Gilbert composed a letter to his father in his mind. The light in the kitchen window stopped him. Pa was still awake. Gilbert couldn't face him.

Gilbert tiptoed to the door and pulled it open a crack. A single candle flickered on the table. Pa must have gone to bed. Before Gilbert lost his courage, he took the candle to hunt pencil and paper to write a letter.

Pa,

You and I can't agree. I meant what I said about school. I'm leaving to be on my own.

Your son, Gilbert

PS. Old Herman says to ask him for help if you need it.

Gilbert took a gunnysack to his room and collected a blanket, a change of clothes, an extra pair of shoes, and his knife. He lifted the loose board under his bed and found the six dollars he'd earned by harvest work for neighbors. He stopped by the pantry and stowed a loaf of bread and a chunk of cheese in the sack.

Pilot nudged his leg, and Gilbert bent down to stroke his dog's head. "You wonder what I'm doing here when I should be sleeping? I wonder, too."

Pilot pushed his nose out the door when Gilbert tried to leave. Gilbert blocked him with his leg. "Stay, Pilot." The dog whimpered and gave him a forlorn look. Gilbert looked quickly away, toughening his heart, and closed the door behind him.

Without a backward glance he strode into the pale moonlight and headed toward Westerville.

3
Twenty Questions

Gilbert sat up and rubbed the sleep out of his eyes. A terrible stink had awakened him from a sound sleep. Skunk! He tried to remember where he was. It took a minute to gather the clues. He had run through pouring rain and climbed the ladder to a hayloft to escape from a snarling dog.

He knew he'd smell like a skunk if he stayed in the stranger's barn another minute. He stood and brushed straw from his damp clothes and combed his fingers through his dark brown hair so he wouldn't look like a hayseed. He shouldered his gunnysack, climbed down the ladder. As the first streaks of dawn colored the sky, he headed toward town.

When Westerville loomed in the distance, he sat down for a rest. Gilbert knew a little about Westerville from shopping there with his parents, so he formed a plan. Find a place to stay and hunt for a job.

As Gilbert walked the wooden sidewalks, church bells chimed. At home, Pa would be going to church by himself. Everyone would ask lots of questions.

Gilbert tilted his head to hear the singing from the Methodist church further along State Street. The hymn was one they sang at his church back home. He crept to the open door and slipped into the back row as the congregation finished the last verse.

~ Choosing Sides ~

From the back pew he had a good view of the worshipers. The crowd was twice the size of his own church and the ladies' hats had more flowers and feathers. The preacher at the front told everyone to open his Bible to John, chapter 15. Gilbert looked around, hoping nobody noticed he didn't have a Bible.

The preacher read about a man with two sons. One son ran away instead of helping his father on the farm. This made Gilbert slide lower in the pew. He wondered how the preacher knew he would be there this morning.

The son wasted all his inheritance money on wild living. The preacher told how hungry the boy got—hungry enough to eat the food he was feeding to the pigs. None of the boy's friends gave him anything to eat, and he nearly starved.

Gilbert looked around to see if anyone else knew the preacher's sermon was about him, but nobody returned his look. One man was asleep, judging by the way his head tilted and his mouth hung open.

The preacher had good news about the son, Gilbert guessed by his raised voice and the extra arm-waving. "That boy had to get to the end of his rope before he woke up to how foolish he had been. His first step was admitting to himself he had sinned against God. Next he decided to return home and beg his father's forgiveness."

The preacher looked right at Gilbert. "How many of you have sinned against someone? Are you ready to ask his forgiveness?" Gilbert wanted to run out the door, but he slid lower and stayed rooted to his seat. He argued with himself over whether he was wrong to leave the farm. He tried convincing himself he didn't leave for a bad reason, but a good one. An inner voice demanded to know, "Why did you leave at night without speaking to your father?"

Gilbert felt his face get red. The preacher continued preaching, but Gilbert didn't hear much more. He determined to get out of church as quickly as possible. When everyone stood to sing the final hymn, he put the hymnal back in the rack and slipped to the end of the pew.

Before he could get out the door, a bulky man in a suit and tie blocked his way, extending his hand to Gilbert. “Good morning, young man. We’re glad to see you here today. My name is L.P. Goodspeed. May I ask yours?”

Gilbert shook hands, trying to squeeze back hard enough so his own hand wouldn’t be crushed. “My name’s Gilbert. Gilbert Freeman.”

“Ah, you must be Theodore Freeman’s son. Your family has shopped at my store, right there on State Street. I deal in hardware and agricultural implements.”

The man did look familiar. Gilbert concentrated on remembering and smiled when he connected the man’s face with his store, but he hesitated at Mr. Goodspeed’s next question. “What brings you to Westerville?”

Gilbert thought of a good answer, even if it missed part of the reason. “I-I’m looking for a job.”

“You look like a hard worker, young man. Someone will hire you.” Mr. Goodspeed rubbed his chin. “You know, we have a roast simmering at home, with all the fixings, and one more person is what we need to make our table complete. Will you join us for dinner?”

Gilbert’s face brightened, and he grinned. “Thank you, Mr. Goodspeed. I would like that.”

“Of course. I’m getting hungry too, after that sermon and all the talk about a starving boy. Come meet my family, and we’ll be on our way.”

The Goodspeed family lived in a brick house in town. A rugged maple tree shaded the yard, and red geraniums bloomed in flower boxes lining the porch. Mrs. Goodspeed and their two daughters, Rose and Iva, bustled about in the kitchen getting the meal ready. Gilbert tried to hold up his end of the conversation with Mr. Goodspeed and even asked questions of his own.

~ Choosing Sides ~

When everyone was seated for the meal, Gilbert sat beside Rose and across from Iva. Rose's smile gave him a buzzy feeling inside. Her blonde hair reminded him of how his mother had worn her hair, swept up into a circle on top of her head.

Mr. Goodspeed prayed a blessing on the food and then tucked a napkin under his chin. "Let's get this meal underway." He handed Gilbert the platter of meat, followed by a bowl of mashed potatoes and the gravy boat.

Mrs. Goodspeed watched Gilbert take small helpings of everything. "That's not enough for a growing boy. There's plenty, so fill your plate."

"Thank you, Ma'am." Gilbert piled on the carrots and took three dinner rolls.

Mr. Goodspeed served himself a generous helping of everything. "Your father is a longtime customer of mine. He's a top-notch farmer."

Mrs. Goodspeed asked, "Where is your farm?"

Gilbert remembered his manners and finished his bite before answering. "Freeman farm is about six miles north of here."

Mrs. Goodspeed said, "We were terribly sorry to hear about your mother."

Gilbert had feared they'd ask about his mother and then his feelings might burst out of control. He swallowed hard and mumbled what he hoped was the right answer. "Yes, Ma'am."

Rose came to his rescue and offered the jar of jam. "Be sure to try this on your rolls. Mama's strawberry jam is the best."

Iva flipped her braids back and forth. "We're going to pick strawberries tomorrow so Mama can make more jam."

Rose spread jam on her roll and asked Gilbert, "Do you have any sisters?"

"Only one, Annie. She's two years younger than me."

Iva stuck out her lower lip. "I wish I had a younger sister instead of an older sister. Then I wouldn't get bossed around. Or have to wear hand-me-downs."

Mrs. Goodspeed narrowed her gaze. "Mind your manners, Iva."

Rose smirked at her sister, then asked their guest a question. "What's Annie doing this summer?"

"She's staying with our aunt in Mt. Vernon." Gilbert guessed she was having a good time.

Mr. Goodspeed nodded toward a framed photo. "Did you notice the photo behind you?"

Gilbert shook his head and turned to see. Glaring back at him from a framed photograph was an older woman with a somber look.

"That's Mother Stewart." Mrs. Goodspeed said.

Gilbert had never heard of Mother Stewart.

Mr. Goodspeed watched Gilbert's reaction. "She successfully fought the liquor trade by leading Temperance Marches all over Ohio. We were honored to have her share a Sunday dinner with us two years ago."

Mrs. Goodspeed glowed as she spoke of the great event in their home. "Mother Stewart also spoke at Mass Temperance Rallies. We went to one and pleaded with her to come home and dine with us."

Mr. Goodspeed beamed at his girls. "Since our girls are growing up—Rose is thirteen and Iva is eleven—we wanted them to meet Mother Stewart, who has had such great influence for good."

Gilbert glanced at Rose, who wrinkled her nose. Iva's head moved back and forth, but only a little. He wondered if the girls agreed with their parents.

After dinner, Mrs. Goodspeed shooed them all to the parlor. Mr. Goodspeed sat in an overstuffed chair to read his newspaper and soon fell asleep. The girls perched on the loveseat with their large tiger cat between them. Rose stroked the cat, and it purred.

Gilbert asked, "What's his name?"

"Her name is Ginger." Rose stroked Ginger and grinned at Gilbert. "Do you know how to play Twenty Questions?"

"Sure. Annie and I play it all the time."

"You can be first," Rose said. Gilbert took it as a challenge to think of something hard to guess.

He stared at the patterned wallpaper for a while. "I'm thinking of something yellow."

"Is it alive?" Iva asked.

"No."

"Is it bigger than a cat?" Rose asked.

"No."

"Is it something to play with?" Iva asked.

"No."

"Did you see this at our house?" Rose asked.

"No." Gilbert grinned and bent four fingers down.

Iva grabbed her sister's arm. "You have to think of better questions. We can't let a boy beat us."

Rose raised her eyebrows. "Is it something to eat?"

"Yes." Gilbert tried not to smile.

"Did we have it at dinner today?" Iva's question came upon the heels of her sister's.

"No." Gilbert bent down two more fingers.

"Hmm." Iva twirled the cat's tail around her finger. "We don't know what you've been eating, Gilbert. No fair."

"Did I say I ate it? Maybe a horse eats it." Gilbert tried to conceal the smile trying to push through.

Rose pounced on the hint. "Does a horse eat it?"

"Nope." Gilbert bent one more finger down.

Iva frowned. "That was a dumb question." She thought a while and asked, "Does any animal eat it?"

"Maybe."

"Yes or no." Rose crossed her arms. "Maybe is not allowed."

"All right. Yes, a certain animal eats it." Gilbert shook his head, since the answer might be misleading. He counted off another question. "Twelve questions left."

"Does the animal live in a house?"

Gilbert bent another finger down. "Yes. But not all the time."

Iva jumped to her feet. "Is it a pet?"

Gilbert grinned. "No." He bent another finger down. "Ten questions left."

Rose's face got redder as she and Iva asked eight more questions without getting a "yes" answer.

Iva chanted to her sister, "Temper, temper, don't lose your temper. Or else you'll have to go to a temperance meeting."

Rose glared at her sister.

Gilbert smiled to himself, thinking of times when Annie taunted him. "You went to the Mother Stewart meetings—what were they like?"

Iva glanced at her sleeping father and lowered her voice. "Yes, we had to go to Mother Stewart's meetings. And temperance meetings at our church. And meetings at other churches."

Rose kept her voice to a whisper. "Most of them were long and boring. We got everlastingly tired of temperance meetings."

"I'd get tired of them, too."

"We had to be quiet as a mouse," Rose said.

Iva jumped up, forgetting to be quiet. "A mouse! A mouse is what eats the yellow food."

Mr. Goodspeed sat up, blinking. "A mouse is in the house?"

"No, Papa. I'm sorry," Iva said. "We were playing a game,"

Rose grinned at Gilbert. "It's cheese, isn't it."

"Yes, you guessed it just in time. That was your last question." Gilbert was glad they'd figured out the answer. He hoped to be invited back.

When it was time to leave, Gilbert thanked Mr. Goodspeed for inviting him and thanked Mrs. Goodspeed for the delicious dinner.

"You must come again, promise?" Mrs. Goodspeed said.

Rose stepped outside the door with Gilbert to send him on his way. "You have to come again. We don't have a chance to talk about temperance to someone who lets us think for ourselves." She touched his arm, blushed, and ran back into the house.

Gilbert decided he would spend the night in another barn. He walked out of town about a mile, ignoring the first two barns. One was too close to the farmer's house and the other had a fierce dog barking to warn trespassers to stay away from his territory. The third barn had no guard dog and was across the field from the farmhouse, so he ducked inside and climbed into the hayloft. He watched a pink and purple sunset from the open window. The shadows lengthened and the lightning bugs blinked in the field behind the barn.

As he remembered Rose's goodbye, Gilbert got a warm feeling. He thought about all the temperance meetings the Goodspeed girls had to sit through. At least his parents didn't drag him to that kind of thing. He imagined how worried his father must be about his runaway son. Remembering the sermon from the morning brought a stab of guilt, which he quickly drove out of his mind. Tomorrow he'd see about a job and about a room to rent. If he failed . . . well, he wouldn't fail!

4
A Room to Rent

Next morning Gilbert went to the Little Bonanza Restaurant for breakfast. He remembered eating there with his parents in the past. His bread and cheese would have to wait.

"Good morning, son." The man behind the counter gave him a friendly smile. Two other men in work clothes nodded a greeting to him, too.

Gilbert perched on the last stool in the row. "Hello, sir. What's the cheapest breakfast?"

"A ham sandwich for five cents. Or three boiled eggs be just seven cents."

Gilbert thought they both sounded good. "I'll take the sandwich, please."

His sandwich came with a cup of lukewarm tea, which Gilbert downed right away. The man smiled and filled it again. "You be mighty early to town, young man. How come?"

"I'm looking for a room to rent. And a job."

"Whew! That be a tall order." The man wiped the counter and stared out the dirty window. "Not many jobs around here. 'Cause of the big panic two years ago."

Gilbert gobbled the sandwich and emptied his cup of tea again. "Know anyone who would rent me a room? A cheap room."

"Maybe. Master Conkle—he and two young fellas rent a house together." The man refilled Gilbert's cup. "Head down Main Street toward Alum Creek, then out West Street toward the edge of town. A white house, or at least it used to be, and it sets right where the road curves."

Gilbert dug a nickel from his gunnysack. "Thanks for the tip, sir." He headed down Main Street to find the house. The towers of Otterbein's new administration building loomed in the distance, and he stopped to stare. It was such a grand building he felt drawn to go inside.

He gawked like a sightseer at the arched doorways and ornate woodwork. Framed photographs of the previous graduating classes lined the hallway. The young men, hair neatly combed, appeared formal and serious in their high collars. The young ladies, attractive in their upswept hairdos, looked nothing like most of the girls he knew. He stared at a portrait of the president of the college. His smiling eyes reminded Gilbert of Pa, the way he looked before Ma died.

Heading down West Street again, Gilbert searched for the house he'd heard about at the restaurant. He edged between muddy ruts and around large puddles. When he found the house, a two story with peeling white paint, he knocked on the door, wondering what kind of person would answer.

A gray cat rubbed against his leg. The cat made him feel welcome, and he reached down and petted it. Someone inside shouted for him to come on in. The cat followed at his heels.

Gilbert grimaced at the piles of newspapers, empty boxes, and scrap lumber piled in the entry hall. He turned right and entered a parlor with a black stove perched on a brick hearth. In the far corner, a husky young man in his mid-twenties sprawled in a wing-back chair. He jumped up when he saw Gilbert.

"Ho! I thought . . . oh, never mind," the man said. "What do you want?"

"The man at Little Bonanza said you might have a room to rent."

"Oh. Maybe we do. What's your name?"

"Gilbert Freeman."

"Mine's Frederick Conkle. But call me Freddie. Three of us share the rent. One more would make it cheaper."

"I can't afford much, till I find a job. How much for the rent?"

"We'll give you the first month free. That way if we don't like you . . . ." Freddie laughed. "I'm joking. If you can put up with us, we can put up with you."

"Can I look around?"

"Sure. I'll give you the grand tour." Freddie reached down to pet the cat. "Meet Shadow, our friendly and faithful mouser." He headed through an arched doorway. "Here's the kitchen, a bit messy right now." He waved his hand at a table piled with pots and a sink stacked with dishes. "We don't use the cook-stove often—we work all day."

Gilbert winced at the clutter and dirt. He could hear Annie's disapproving voice.

As they passed a back window, Freddie said, "We keep a few chickens in the coop out there."

"Chickens . . . we have a flock on our farm." Gilbert again thought of Annie, the official keeper of the chickens at Free-man Farm.

Freddie grinned. "What's a farm boy doing in town?".

Gilbert started to answer, but Freddie continued the tour. "The privy's out back. And there's the dining room, but we don't eat there much." Gilbert glimpsed a cluttered table with four chairs, and a desk in the corner littered with papers.

Freddie waved his hand at two closed doors. "Benjie and I have the two bedrooms on the main floor." They climbed a narrow, creaky stairway. "Vern has a room here on the second floor."

Gilbert peered down the hall. "I see two doors, so one must be the empty one."

"Yep. The room on the left can be for you."

When he pushed the door open, it bumped into a narrow bed. A chair, a table, and rickety dresser completed the furniture. The stuffiness of the room made Gilbert gasp, so he strode to the window and wrestled it open. The fresh air poured in, and he leaned out to see how far he could see down West Street.

"Well, is this room worth a dollar and twenty cents a month?" Freddie grinned. "We might even give you a discount for the smallest room."

Gilbert tried to ignore his negative thoughts about the trash downstairs. The room was dusty, but clean enough otherwise. "Yes, I'll pay that. You all will have to help me find my way around town, too."

"Don't worry. We'll teach you plenty!" Freddie laughed and headed back down the stairs.

Gilbert perched on the bed. Shadow hopped beside him and purred. What lay ahead for him now he'd left behind Pa and the farm?

5
New Venture

The next day, Gilbert set out to find a job. The houses on West Street had neat yards. That meant they didn't need to hire anyone to do yard work. He headed toward Main Street—the Presbyterian Church had a buggy parked behind it. Churches had their own members to clean the building, so he didn't stop.

Ahead, a middle-aged man and woman were dragging trash from a brick building. Gilbert ran to catch them before they went back inside. "Mister, sir, I see you're working hard there. Do you need any help?"

The woman looked at him as if he might be a spy. "Are you connected to Otterbein?"

"No, Ma'am." Gilbert looked at the man, hoping he'd want to hire him.

The man shook his head. "We don't want word of our new venture getting out until we're ready to open. Competition, you know."

Gilbert said, "I'm a stranger from out of town. I'd keep your secret."

The woman adjusted her scarf, showing her black hair. "Our work needs strong arms." She studied Gilbert, making him conscious of his slender frame.

Gilbert puffed out his chest. "I've worked on our farm, lifting bales of hay, carrying boxes of apples . . . ."

The man and woman exchanged glances. The woman gave a slight nod, though she didn't look convinced.

The man said, "We will hire you for the day, to see how well you do. What's your name?"

"Gilbert Freeman. I'll work for you as long as you need me."

"I'm Harry Corbin and this is my wife. She'll give you directions about what she wants you to do."

Gilbert nodded. "Pleased to meet you, Ma'am."

Mrs. Corbin's smile looked forced. She nodded but wasted no time on pleasantries. "This building is full of trash. Get to work hauling it out back so Mr. Corbin can burn it."

Mr. Corbin led the way inside and helped Gilbert collect rags, papers, and broken furniture from the three rooms. When the pile behind the building had grown waist-high, Mr. Corbin lit a match. As he watched the clouds of black smoke billowing down Main Street, he also lit himself a cigarette.

When Gilbert brought the next load of trash, Mr. Corbin confronted an angry neighbor. The man waved his arms and shouted, "Put out this fire! Your smoke is blowing into my house and it stinks."

Swearing, Mr. Corbin shook his fist in the man's face. The man turned on his heel and stomped back home. Gilbert disappeared back inside.

When Gilbert had finished with the trash, Mrs. Corbin handed him a broom. "Start in the back room. Here's a dustpan." Dust filled the air as she swept the main room. Gilbert sneezed once, but Mrs. Corbin sneezed three times. Gilbert tried not to stare when she wiped her nose on a corner of her headscarf.

Twice Gilbert filled the dustpan and emptied it out back. Every time he thought he was done, Mrs. Corbin found more dirt for him to sweep.

Mr. Corbin, smelling of smoke, poked his head in the door. "I'm ready for lunch. Our trash pile can finish smoldering without my help." He snickered. "I told off that grouchy neighbor. Maybe he'll put out the fire for us."

Gilbert stopped sweeping and held his stomach. It growled from missing breakfast.

Hands on hips, Mrs. Corbin glared at her husband. "Do we have to stop our progress? We've—"

Mr. Corbin cut in. "We're going to lunch. Now." He swore an oath to prove how hungry he was. "Come on, Gilbert."

Over sandwiches at the Little Bonanza, Mr. Corbin planned the afternoon jobs. "We need to buy paint for those three rooms."

Mrs. Corbin shook her head. "We can't paint until we wash those filthy walls." She shoved in a bite of sandwich and kept talking. "And mopping the floors comes next."

Mr. Corbin guessed they would need the rest of the day to finish cleaning. "You can come and work tomorrow."

"Yes, sir, Mr. Corbin."

Mrs. Corbin stood. "You had your food. Let's get back to work."

During the rest of the afternoon Gilbert mopped the floors and helped wash the walls. He carried a set of grimy wooden chairs outside to remove layers of dirt. When he carried them back inside, Mr. Corbin perched on one to test it, and it tilted at a dangerous angle. "I'll tighten these, or my customers might fall on the floor." Gilbert guessed their business might be a cafe.

Mrs. Corbin pushed against the table. "Fix this, too—the front leg wobbles."

Mr. Corbin whipped out a little book and penciled a list. "Screws and glue to fix table and chairs. Brushes and paint for walls. Long boards and supports for a bar and shelves."

"Don't forget, we'll need a sign, so buy a board and paint for that, too." Mrs. Corbin scanned the room. "We've made real progress today. Gilbert, I have to admit you're a hard worker."

Harry reached into his pocket. "Here's your pay. See you tomorrow at eight, sharp."

Gilbert's mouth dropped open when he saw the silver dollar. "Thank you, sir. I'll see you then."

6
Gilbert's New Title

Before going back to the house on West Street, Gilbert walked around town. He admired Westerville's three large churches—Presbyterian, Methodist, and United Brethren. The churches reminded him of home and his little white church where everyone knew everyone else. He remembered church suppers and Sunday School picnics. He headed toward West Street.

As he stepped onto the porch, Gilbert heard his new housemates laughing. He hurried inside to see what was going on.

"Hey, it's Gilbert." Freddie stood and pulled him into the parlor. Two other young men in their mid-twenties lounged on the furniture and ate from plates on their laps. Their dirty work clothes revealed how they'd spent the day. Shadow jumped beside one and tasted his meal. Gilbert inhaled the delicious aroma of their supper—pork and beans—and realized how hungry he was.

Freddie introduced Gilbert around the room and brought him a plate of beans and a fork. "Benjie was telling how he duped our boss at work. Neither of us like the guy. The best part is, he'll never figure out Benjie did it."

Vern, whose thin face and hooked nose reminded Gilbert of a hawk, waved his fork. "We need to plan more stunts. Any ideas?"

Gilbert listened as he downed his beans, aghast at their schemes. He laughed at the prank ideas, like turning over an outhouse, but when the plans included explosives, he shook his head.

Freddie said, "Gil doesn't approve of our clever plans." Gilbert started to say why, but Freddie interrupted. "Tell us about your day—your clothes look as dirty as ours."

"I worked for a man and his wife, cleaning out a building they rented on Main Street. It was filthy and full of trash. I'm going back tomorrow to help paint."

"Not bad, finding a job so fast." Benjie, short and stocky, had dark curly hair and a crooked grin. "So why did you leave home? You probably had a soft bed and someone to cook your meals there."

Gilbert felt a twinge of sadness. He didn't feel like telling these fellows why he'd run away. He spooned a second helping of beans and settled back on his wooden chair. "I'll be going to school in town this fall. That's all."

Low whistles greeted this news, and Freddie hooted. "Gil may be smart, but he's got a few things to learn."

"Like how to pull good pranks?" Vern laughed.

"Or how to do as little work as possible and still get paid?" Benjie said.

Gilbert chuckled. "Like the best place to buy meat and bread."

Freddie's expression changed. "We have a hard time shopping, working ten-hour days. I happened to be here this morning when you came, 'cause I took a half-day off. For personal reasons."

Vern licked his lips. "Maybe you can buy groceries for the rest of us."

Benjie rubbed his stomach and asked, "Are you any good at cooking?"

"I'm not *good*, but I know how to make meat-n-potato meals." Gilbert thought of the times he and Annie had made supper after their mother died.

Freddie slapped Gilbert on the back. "I nominate Gil as our chief cook."

Gilbert thought hard about the idea and bit his lip. "Shopping and cooking is work." He grinned. "I'll do it—if it counts as my rent."

Freddie looked to the others, and they all agreed. "You're officially hired."

Vern looked down his hooked nose. "Shouldn't he have a trial period?"

Benjie asked, "How soon can you start?"

"We can figure out the details after Gilbert gets settled," Freddie said.

That night, Gilbert got ready for bed in the dark and realized he should have brought candles. He lay awake, still amazed he'd found a place to live and a job so soon. He figured God must be watching out for him, even though he hadn't asked.

7
Painting the Sign

Gilbert woke to the patter of rain on the roof. He leaned out the open window to let the drops hit his face, like he used to do at home. The rain smelled like earthworms in town, not the clean fresh-cut hay smell of the farm. He wondered how Pa was doing with the chores. He dressed in his work clothes and tried not to think how hungry he was.

Downstairs, Gilbert saw no sign of his housemates. He strained to remember their names—Freddie, Vern, and Benjie. Outside, Shadow bounded toward him and purred when Gilbert stroked him. He pretended it was Pilot, since otherwise he'd feel disloyal to his faithful dog.

A light rain spritzed his face, but the gray clouds threatened heavier rain to come. He stepped along the edge of West Street, avoiding the worst of the mud.

Gilbert spotted the Corbin's brick building in the distance when the clouds opened and poured sheets of rain. He ran the last hundred yards, ignoring the muddy fountains his shoes made in the puddles. Glad to get out of the rain, he ducked inside the Corbin building.

Mrs. Corbin, her face like a storm cloud, glared at the trail of mud behind him. "There goes all our work from yesterday."

Gilbert wiped his face on his sleeve and gulped. “I’m sorry. I’ll mop it again, Mrs. Corbin.”

Mr. Corbin came in the front door with an armload of tools, making another muddy trail. When his wife lectured him, he cut her short. “Just shut up. When we have customers, they’ll track in mud, too.”

Mrs. Corbin spat an order to Gilbert. “Don’t bother mopping till the end of the day.”

Mr. Corbin peered out at the rain. “I have more things to unload from the wagon. It better stop raining soon.”

Mrs. Corbin waved her hand. “Take the umbrella and go shop for paint. The cheapest white paint will work.”

“How many gallons?” He looked around at the walls. “These ugly walls may take two coats.”

She glanced around the three rooms. “Two gallons. We can thin it if we run out.”

Gilbert and Mr. Corbin headed into the rain, and Mrs. Corbin called out more purchases. “Buy brushes, two wide ones. A narrow brush for lettering the sign. And black paint.”

After Mr. Corbin and Gilbert returned with the supplies, they began painting in the back room. Gilbert dripped trails of paint on the floor.

Mrs. Corbin glared at the mess and tossed him rags. “Don’t drip all over the place.”

While they painted, Mr. Corbin gabbed. “We ran a hardware store in Westerville five years ago.”

“I grew up on a farm.” Gilbert swabbed at a row of drips.

Mr. Corbin glanced at his wife. “We’ve got five children, and our youngest is two. They’re at home with their grandma.”

“I’ve got a younger sister.” Gilbert wondered if Annie would laugh to see him spattered with white paint.

“My children are growing up fast.” Mr. Corbin stood on tiptoe to reach the high section of wall. “If this new business thrives, I plan to hand it along to my oldest boy. He’s nine.”

Gilbert said, "I'll be in ninth grade." Gilbert wondered if he'd go to school with the Corbin children. Did Westerville have a one-room schoolhouse like in the country? He'd rather attend Otterbein's Academy, since it prepared a student for college. But that cost money.

After they finished the first coat for all three rooms, Mr. Corbin peered out the window. "It quit raining, looks like. Let's unload the wagon." Gilbert wiped paint off his hands and followed him out the door.

The wagon had half a dozen lengths of planking, a pile of bricks, and a wooden box of tools, all under a canvas cover. First, Mr. Corbin and Gilbert tackled the longest and heaviest plank. Gilbert stepped backward through the mud, gripping the plank with all his strength. All at once, both feet slipped out from under him and the plank crashed against his shin and landed on his foot.

"Oww!" Gilbert tried to shove the end of the plank off his foot to relieve the pain in his toe.

Mr. Corbin knelt beside him and lifted it out of the way. "You all right? Did it hit your leg?"

Gilbert nodded.

Mr. Corbin felt along Gilbert's shin.

Gilbert winced.

"I don't think it's broken," Mr. Corbin said.

"But I think my toe is." Gilbert tried to stand, but Mr. Corbin held him down.

"Sit still. Let me take a look." He rolled up Gilbert's pant leg. The scraped skin was bleeding. "Hmm. We need to clean that wound and bandage it."

Mrs. Corbin came out and peered down at Gilbert. "It's only a little scrape. Harry, get him off this damp ground and help him inside. Then I'll wrap a rag around his leg."

Gilbert limped inside supported between the two of them and settled on a pile of clean rags. "What can we do about your toe?" Mr. Corbin asked.

"Not much you can do for it. Don't worry about me—I'll be all right."

After Mrs. Corbin had cleaned and bandaged his leg, Gilbert felt well enough to ask her for a job to do. She brought the black paint and a narrow brush. "Our sign needs a steady hand to paint the letters. Think you can do it? I don't want any black blobs."

Gilbert tilted his head. He had no experience painting letters, but the job didn't sound too hard. "I'll do my best, Mrs. Corbin."

"I've drawn the letters in pencil, you fill them in."

Gilbert perched on his rag pile and braced the board on his lap. He guided the brush close to the edge of the pencil line instead of dabbing to fill in the letters.

Mrs. Corbin paced back and forth. "When will we hang our sign?"

Mr. Corbin looked up from writing in the expense ledger. "Hold off as long as possible. You know folks will raise a ruckus."

Gilbert had finished painting C-O-R-B-. He wondered why anyone would be upset over another restaurant.

Mrs. Corbin narrowed her gaze. "I thought we'd open tomorrow."

"No, day after." Mr. Corbin bent to check Gilbert's work. "We'll hang the sign tomorrow, though, and word of mouth will bring in the customers."

Mrs. Corbin smirked at her husband. "Westerville has a big surprise coming."

Gilbert kept painting. He was curious as to what came next, so he bent to read the penciled letters—S-A-L-O-O-N. The realization hit him hard, and he nearly toppled over backward. The Corbins were opening a saloon! What would his father think? What would Aunt Ruby think?

Gilbert tried to keep painting, but his hand shook. He called out to Mr. Corbin. "I-I feel dizzy, sir. Maybe it's from the board falling on my leg. Or from the paint fumes."

Mrs. Corbin peered at him. "You do look pale. Harry, let's break for lunch and get Gilbert food and fresh air."

Mr. Corbin chuckled. "You've learned a good lesson, Mrs. Corbin—we men regard food as a cure-all."

Mr. Corbin helped Gilbert stand. "Can you hobble to Little Bonanza if we help?" Gilbert's leg ached and his toe throbbed, so he nodded.

They sat at a wobbly table near the window and ordered ham sandwiches. As soon as the waitress was out of earshot, Mr. Corbin said, "What I wouldn't give for a cold beer."

Mrs. Corbin rolled her eyes. "What did you expect in a dry town?"

Mr. Corbin grinned and took a big bite of sandwich. "Gilbert, you done for the day?"

Gilbert opened his mouth to answer when Mrs. Corbin answered for him. "The best thing for him would be to prop his leg on a pillow for the rest of the day. He's not worth much if he can't walk. Pay him for his work this morning."

Mr. Corbin handed him a fifty-cent piece, and he put it in his pocket. He felt for the silver dollar from the day before, but it was not there. He reached deeper and felt the frayed edges of a hole. Gilbert groaned to himself but tried to smile as he thanked Mr. Corbin. He switched the new coin to his left pocket, making sure it didn't have a hole, too.

Mr. Corbin delivered Gilbert to the house on West Street. "I hope your leg's better tomorrow so you can come back to work."

Gilbert climbed down from the buggy, favoring his sore leg. "Thank you, sir."

As he watched Mr. Corbin heading back to his saloon, Gilbert wondered if his leg would feel better by tomorrow. Even more, he wondered whether he should return to work. Thinking of what the Corbins were doing gave him a sick feeling in the pit of his stomach.

8
Gilbert's Problem

Gilbert spent the afternoon with his leg propped up on a footstool. His head ached with the knowledge of the Corbins' plans. He wanted to pace around the room to help him think about a plan of action. He missed walking in the pine woods with Pilot beside him, and he wished he could sit on his thinking log.

Instead, Gilbert poured out his problems to Shadow, purring on his lap. "The Corbins are going to open a saloon in Westerville. My father and my aunt would be horrified if they knew I helped a liquor-seller. But Mr. Corbin gave me a job and bought me lunch twice. I don't see what's so bad about selling alcohol. And I have only one more day. Should I go back? I can't let them down, after all they've done to help me."

He closed his eyes, remembering the things he had been taught at home. He could hear his father saying, "Ardent spirits cause poverty, idleness, and crime." Aunt Ruby's voice came next. "Intemperance leads a young man down, down, to an early grave." His mother's voice was quieter. "Please promise me you'll never start imbibing spirits, Gilbert. It would break my heart."

Gilbert marshalled facts for the other side of the question. Shadow listened as well as Pilot. "Uncle Bill drinks beer, and he's an elder in his church. And Old Herman isn't poor or idle.

He earns an honest living by farming. He's at least fifty, pretty old, and he's still alive. Maybe the whole crusade against alcohol is making a mountain out of a molehill. Maybe alcohol isn't that dangerous."

Gilbert dozed off but jerked awake when the front door slammed. Freddie stood in front of him, his lunchbox in one hand and a burlap bag of apples in the other. "Hey, Gilbert. What happened to your leg?"

"Oh, you're back already. I must've slept a couple of hours." He rubbed his injured leg. "I helped Mr. Corbin carry a heavy plank, and I slipped in the mud."

"Too bad. What's this Corbin fellow going to do with the place you're helping him clean and paint?"

"I found out today. He's opening a saloon."

Freddie dropped his jaw and the bag of apples. "A saloon? In Westerville? Are you sure?"

"I painted the sign myself. Well, half of it."

"He's asking for trouble if he brings spirits into this dry town."

"Is there a law against it?" Gilbert hadn't thought about that possibility.

"I don't know if there's a law, but plenty of folks in town would be against it." Freddie bent to grab the apples, which had rolled in all directions. Shadow batted one to the far side of the room.

Gilbert sat up. "Where'd you get the apples?"

"Found them on a tree."

"A tree . . . in an orchard?"

"You ask too many questions."

Vern and Benjie crowded into the room, and Vern barged into the conversation. "Have you made our supper yet?"

Gilbert opened his mouth to answer, but Freddie interrupted. "Of course, he hasn't. Can't you see he's hurt?"

Gilbert tried to stand. "I-I thought you all would give me money to buy groceries and tell me what to cook."

Freddie pulled Gilbert back into the chair. "Sit down. Tomorrow or the next day you can start, if your leg is better. We'll give you shopping money, and you can figure out supper for us each night."

Benjie headed toward the kitchen. "But I'm hungry now."

Vern joined Benjie and helped him open two large cans of pork and beans. "Guess it's beans again."

Freddie raised the bag of apples with a grin. "And these green apples, which I thinned from a tree with too many."

As the young men sat around the parlor eating and gabbing about their day, Vern tested an idea on his buddies. "This guy at work always spins stories about having a ghost in his house—he's really scared of them. Wouldn't it be fun to dress up in white sheets and sneak over to his place tonight?"

"Then tomorrow at work he'd tell you all about the ghost who visited him." Benjie laughed so hard the spoonful of beans missed his mouth. As soon as it hit the floor, Shadow darted to the spot.

Vern poked his hawk-like nose in Benjie's face. "I dare you to come with me."

Benjie smirked. "Do you know where he lives?"

Vern nodded and shoveled in another bite.

Freddie narrowed his eyes and spoke to Gilbert. "Find out everything you can about the saloon and report back."

Gilbert guessed they planned to play a prank on Mr. Corbin, so he didn't say as much as he knew. "They're opening soon."

Vern nodded. "Watch out for fireworks."

Freddie tapped the table. "From the Women's Temperance movement."

Benjie raised his voice. "The whole town of Westerville is a Temperance Movement. They think everyone should abstain from alcohol. Can't say as I agree."

Gilbert decided not to mention his aunt had marched in Temperance parades.

"Temperance marches can't keep me from swigging, even in dry Westerville." Benjie pulled out a flask from his hip pocket. "Want a sip, Vern?"

Vern shook his head at first but changed his mind. "Just a nip, no more."

Freddie glared at Benjie. "My mother marched on a tavern in my hometown of Hillsboro. All the ladies stood in front of the saloon and had a pray-in." Freddie lowered his voice. "Every time I go home for a visit, she tells me she prays for me."

Gilbert thought about his mother. If she were alive, she would be marching with the temperance ladies, too. She'd cry if she knew he'd worked for the Corbins.

Freddie stood and collected Gilbert's empty plate. "There's sure to be a big crowd when Corbin tries to open his saloon. I'm going to take an hour off work to see the excitement." The others said the same thing.

After supper Vern and Benjie left, carrying the white sheets they would wear when they sneaked around the house of Mr. Scared Coworker. Freddie lounged in his favorite chair, reading the newspaper. Gilbert bid Freddie good night and crawled up the stairs to his bedroom. His leg still hurt but he hoped he could work tomorrow.

He flopped on the bed. As he struggled to get comfortable, he thought about what had happened that day. Did God mean to tell him something? He hurt his leg, broke his toe, and lost his silver dollar. Maybe he shouldn't help the Corbins after all.

9

Hanging the Sign

When Gilbert slid out of bed, his leg held his weight and his toe had quit throbbing. After inspecting the dried mud on the back of his pants from the day before, he dressed in his clean pants and a plaid shirt. He wondered how he'd do his laundry. Maybe this house had a wash tub out back. He chewed on the last of the stale bread left in his gunnysack—hard, but better than going hungry.

The others were gone. Gilbert had heard them clomping down the stairs and slamming doors as they left for work. He took a deep breath of the early morning air and half-limped toward town. The Otterbein bells chimed eight times.

He was glad he'd decided to work for the Corbins again today—he'd be there to see any fireworks when they hung their sign. Gilbert saw the Corbin's wagon parked behind their brick building on Main Street as he went inside.

"Good morning, Gilbert. How is your leg feeling today?" Mrs. Corbin's concern seemed genuine, but maybe she wondered which jobs to give him.

"I did what you told me, rested my leg on a pillow all afternoon, and now it's almost back to normal."

- Choosing Sides -

Mr. Corbin swept his hand around the main room. "After you left yesterday, we did a second coat of paint. And see the sturdy bar? I made it from the plank that banged your leg."

Gilbert admired the table and chairs, now glued and braced, sitting near the front window, and the shelves lining three walls. "Looks like you're almost ready to open."

Mrs. Corbin patted the sign. "Almost. I finished the sign, and now we need to hang it."

"And get our stock of liquor." Mr. Corbin stroked his beard. "I've sent word for Edwards to deliver our spirits after dark tonight. If folks spot that delivery wagon in town, they might start a riot."

Gilbert gaped at both of them. They knew the town would be against them, just like Freddie said. "W-When do you plan to open?"

"We'll open tomorrow morning. That's the date on our license." Mr. Corbin stood and walked to the window. "After we hang the sign today, word of mouth will bring in the customers."

Mrs. Corbin narrowed her gaze. "I still wonder if we'll have enough customers. Do you think we'll make a profit running this saloon?"

Mr. Corbin snorted. "I'm not worried. There are folks, even in dry Westerville, who can't stay away from what we'll be selling."

Gilbert thought about Vern. The Corbins planned to make money from people just like him. Vern admitted to Gilbert that once he got started drinking, he couldn't stop.

Mr. Corbin rubbed his hands together. "We might even have a crowd."

Mrs. Corbin looked around the room. "We've got plenty to do. Get that mirror hung."

Mr. Corbin clapped Gilbert on the back. "It's heavy, so I need your help to hang it. I'm glad your leg is better." He led Gilbert to the back room where a long mirror in a wooden frame leaned against the wall. "I've installed the wire hooks behind the bar. You get that end."

The two of them carried it into the main room. Mr. Corbin said, "Don't slip today, young man. Seven years bad luck if you break a mirror."

Gilbert grunted as they lifted the wire over the hooks.

Mr. Corbin adjusted it and stepped back. "Looks good."

Mrs. Corbin handed Gilbert a rag moistened with vinegar water. "I see lots of smudges. Make it shine."

After Gilbert polished the mirror, he unpacked three boxes of glasses. As he swept the floor, he laughed at the colorful prints Mrs. Corbin fixed on the wall—men playing cards and playing tricks on each other.

Mrs. Corbin bit her lip as she looked at the door. "Before the delivery tonight, don't you think we should get a lock for the front door? A thief could walk in and steal whatever they want."

Mr. Corbin scratched his head. "I'll see if Jarvis has a lock at his hardware store. I've been there twenty times the last two days—maybe he'll give me a discount."

Mr. Corbin brought back the lock he had purchased and showed it to Gilbert. "I need to make a large hole for this. Grab my tool bag from the back room."

Mr. Corbin marked a rectangle on the wood under the knob. When he finished drilling a grid of holes, he squared off the edges with a mallet and chisel. One wild swing of the mallet banged his knuckles. He spouted a whole string of swear words. Gilbert had heard language like that once before, from a hired hand on the farm. His father had fired the man the same day.

Mrs. Corbin grimaced at Gilbert. "Harry, watch your language." She hurried to her husband's side. "Maybe Gilbert should finish the job."

Grumbling, Mr. Corbin rubbed his knuckles. "This job won't get the best of me. What if thieves come?" He finished the chiseling and screwed the lock into place. When he tried the key, the bolt clicked. "Success!"

"I'm glad we have a lock—I don't trust this town," said Mrs. Corbin. "What's next on the list?"

Mr. Corbin snickered. "Time to let Westerville see the big change the Corbins are making in their dry town." He lugged the sign from the back room and leaned it against the wall. "Gilbert, bring the big hammer and a handful of nails. I'll get the stepladder."

They dragged the sign outside, and Gilbert stood on two wooden boxes to hold one end, while Mr. Corbin stood on the ladder and nailed in the other end. Gilbert nailed his end of the sign, and they stood back and admired their work. By the time Mrs. Corbin joined them to see how the sign looked, several passers-by stopped and stared.

A farmer in a straw hat asked, "Mister, when is the saloon going to open?"

Mr. Corbin raised his voice so the others nearby could hear. "Tomorrow, July first, we open at nine in the morning to serve this fine community."

More and more people passed by, staring at the new sign. Mr. Corbin stayed outside a while to answer questions.

Mrs. Corbin called Gilbert inside. "We need a card in the window telling our hours. Are you good at printing?"

Gilbert tried to give an honest answer. "My penmanship is . . . not too bad."

She handed him pen, ink, and a white card. "Write this: Hours: 9 a.m. to 8 p.m. daily. Closed on Sunday." When he had finished, she handed him another card and dictated a list of the different beverages and their cost. She propped the first card in the window and tacked the second on the wall behind the bar.

Mr. Corbin dashed in. "Let's go to lunch. I'm hungry, and I bet Gilbert is, too."

"That makes three of us," said Mrs. Corbin.

They headed out, locking the door behind them. Mr. Corbin nodded to the small crowd, even though many glared back. Gilbert felt their stares following him when they walked the two blocks to Little Bonanza.

When they returned from lunch, Gilbert was surprised to see a crowd gathered in front of their building. A woman shouted, "There they are." The three of them rushed inside. Eight men followed them. To Gilbert they looked like important people on serious business.

One man stepped forward to confront the Corbins. "My name is Henry Thompson, President of Otterbein University. I speak for the University, for the pastors of our community, and for the businessmen and townspeople of Westerville. We plead with you not to open a saloon in our town. Westerville has been a dry town since its founding because of our law forbidding the sale of fermented spirits."

Mr. Corbin's piercing black eyes glittered. He straightened his tie and stuck out his chin. "We are going to open tomorrow at nine, no matter what you say."

President Thompson's voice took a harder tone. "Otterbein University has a duty to protect our students from temptation. Please reconsider your decision."

Corbin crossed his arms and set his jaw. "We are law-abiding citizens. Ohio law permits the sale of beer, wine, and ale, and we've obtained a certificate from the state allowing us to serve alcohol. We will serve only pure and wholesome liquor here, as a benefit to this community."

Mrs. Corbin came to stand beside her husband and glared at the intruders. "This dry town needs a saloon, so don't try to stand in our way."

A man with white hair and beard tried a different approach. "Mr. Corbin, my name is Bishop Hanby and I speak for the church of the United Brethren. I don't know if you are a Christian or not, but the Bible has strong words for all of us." Gilbert held his breath, wondering if either one of the Corbins cared what the Bible said. Probably not, he guessed from Mr. Corbin's swearing.

Mr. Hanby drew his brows together and gazed at Mr. Corbin. "Jesus warned us whoever causes one of these little ones who believe in him to sin, it would be better for him if a millstone were hung around his neck, and he were drowned in the depth of the sea. Does this warning put the fear of God into you?"

Corbin lifted his chin and was silent a moment. "I'm sure I'm just as religious as the next man. I don't plan to serve any little ones in my saloon. We'll serve no minors, only those of drinking age."

Mrs. Corbin's face turned red as she listened. She grabbed another chance to speak, and her voice rose almost to a screech. "You better not threaten us any more with your God talk and your local ordinances. Those puny ordinances won't stand up in a court of law. According to Ohio's new law, towns don't have any authority to forbid the sale of alcohol."

Gilbert cringed in a back corner, wishing he were somewhere else. It was awful to hear the Corbins speaking sharp and mean words to these important people. These eight men from Westerville were not making threats, but respectfully asking the Corbins to reconsider.

After the delegation left, Mr. Corbin faced his wife. "I expected this would happen. Don't let it bother you."

Mrs. Corbin straightened her shoulders. "Those holier-than-thou folks make me sick."

Gilbert waited till Mrs. Corbin had cooled down and said, "Those men were sure they were right, and you were wrong, Mr. Corbin. Why is Westerville fighting you so hard?"

Mr. Corbin set his jaw in a hard line. "The temperance crowd is trying to force their rules on everybody. Let each man make up his own mind, I say."

Mrs. Corbin spat her words. "Westerville needs our saloon to shake up the old guard."

"Here's another silver dollar," said Mr. Corbin. "Thanks for coming in today."

Gilbert thanked him and hurried away from the saloon, glad to be gone. He wondered whose side to choose in this battle. President Thompson said he was protecting the students, and Gilbert hoped to be a student in the future. His own family would want him to fight the saloon. But Mr. Corbin said he had Ohio law on his side. Who was right?

He stopped at the bakery to buy bread for supper and ran into Old Herman. "Hello, Mr. Smith. How are you today?"

"Well, if it isn't Gilbert. Your Pa asked me about you."

"Does he know I'm here?"

Old Herman grinned. "Yes, indeed. Though he's none too pleased—he called you his lazy son."

Gilbert bit his lip. "That's not true! I've worked and earned wages. I'm renting a room on West Street."

"I'll tell him I saw you." He looked down State Street. "I came to town to see if the rumors are true, that Westerville is getting a saloon."

Gilbert felt a stab of guilt. "It's true. It's right around the corner on Main Street." He watched Herman head that direction. The Corbins were right—certain people were eager for a saloon, and Old Herman was one of them.

10
Gilbert at Billiards

The aroma of beef stew wafted through the house when Gilbert's housemates came home from work.

Benjie dipped a spoon in the pot for a taste. "You passed the trial period. This meal's a feast."

Gilbert wished Annie could hear the words of praise. She was learning cooking skills from Aunt Ruby, but he learned the hard way, by trial and error.

Freddie patted Gilbert on the back. "We'll all chip in so you can keep fixing supper for us." He collected a dollar from the other two fellows and added his own. "See how far you can make this go toward meat and potatoes and vegetables."

Gilbert stuffed them in his pocket "Three dollars. Are you sure you want to trust me with all this money?"

"We know where you live," Freddie said.

Vern asked, "Is your job with the Corbins finished?"

Gilbert nodded.

Freddie asked, "Isn't tomorrow the day they open?"

"Yep. They open their doors at nine."

Freddie bit into a green apple. "Hmm, I predict there will be a welcoming committee."

Gilbert peered at him, trying to decide if he planned a prank.

After dinner, Vern tapped Gilbert. "Do you know how to play billiards?"

"No, I grew up on a farm."

"We'll teach you." Benjie put his arm on Gilbert's shoulder. "Billiards provides both entertainment and exercise."

Vern peered down his long nose. "Come along with Benjie and me tonight. We're taking the train to Columbus to our favorite billiards parlor."

Gilbert hesitated, wondering what Pa would say. "Sure. As long as it's not expensive."

Benjie chuckled. "Free is even better. My treat tonight."

They walked from the train station to Spook's Bar and Billiards. The cigarette smoke filled the small place like early morning fog. It had so many customers Gilbert wondered if they'd get a chance to play. While they waited, Benjie reached for his wallet. "I'll buy you both a beer so we can enjoy the evening in style."

Vern bit his lip. "You know I'm trying to stay sober." He took three steps backward. "Don't tempt me."

Gilbert shook his head. "No, thanks. I came to learn how to play billiards."

Benjie ignored Vern's plea and came back with two beers, their foam spilling over the side. "Don't be a wet blanket, Vern—I need a drinking buddy."

Gilbert, Vern, and Benjie joined a crowd of men watching a billiards match between a grizzled older man and a slender boy who could barely reach the middle of the table. Benjie explained the finer points of the game as they watched.

"Our turn to play," Benjie said. He set down his beer so he could coach Gilbert. "Aim the cue ball to hit right here." He pointed to the front of a group of billiard balls at the other end of the table.

After missing twice, Gilbert connected stick to cue ball. "Ha! I did it." The clack of the breaking balls as they spun apart made Gilbert grin.

– Choosing Sides –

As the game progressed Benjie and Vern went back to the bar several times. Gilbert wondered if that had anything to do with his surprise win in their third game. "If I keep practicing, watch out."

On the way to the train station, Vern clapped him on the back. "You won a game tonight. Not bad for a first-time player."

"I enjoyed playing, but not the atmosphere."

Vern rubbed his chin. "You mean all the smoke?"

"That, and all the swearing." Gilbert slowed down as the walkway became crowded.

Benjie elbowed his friend. "But how did you like the match that was going on? Those two players are so good they earn money playing billiards."

Gilbert raised his eyebrows. "How? They bet on games?"

"It's—" Benjie didn't get to answer. All three stopped, unable to move forward. The sidewalk ahead overflowed with men and women leaving an event.

Five or six rowdies in black shirts taunted the well-dressed crowd. "Want a drink? I'll share my bottle!"

Gilbert glimpsed one of the signs hung inside the hall. "It's a Temperance Rally."

Benjie raised his voice to add another catcall to what the rowdies shouted. "Hypocrites! How many swigs do you take when nobody's looking?"

Gilbert wished Benjie would stop heckling. He shrank back, afraid someone from the rally might recognize him. When he spotted Mr. and Mrs. Goodspeed, Rose and Iva, he ducked into the shadows behind a husky man in a tall hat.

He decided to disappear, hoping they hadn't seen him. The jeers and catcalls of the crowd faded as Gilbert ran through back alleys. When two men blocked his way, Gilbert raced the opposite direction, fearing he might be beaten and robbed. After many wrong turns, he spotted the train station, and he shouted and waved to his friends.

Vern put his hands on his hips. "There you are."

Benjie drew his brows together. "I thought you'd been kidnapped. What happened?"

Gilbert waited until he caught his breath. "You heckled my friends." He pulled at his collar. "They are not phonies."

Benjie's eyes widened. "You know some of those temperance folks?"

"Yes, I do. Mr. and Mrs. Goodspeed and their daughters Rose and Iva. They've been very kind to me."

Benjie shook his head. "Maybe your friends are different. But most teetotalers try to make everyone follow their rules. A drink now and then doesn't hurt anyone."

Vern held up his hand, as if to stop a wrong statement. "Maybe that's a good motto for you, but it doesn't work for me."

Gilbert felt a stab of guilt. Vern would be another customer for the Corbin Saloon.

11
Opening Day

After his housemates left for work, Gilbert grabbed his gunnysack to use as a grocery bag and headed toward town. At Redding and Clark's Grocery he bought potatoes, onions, and carrots. At Waters and Woods' Meat Market, he purchased a four-pound pork roast. He decided which meat to buy after watching the other shoppers. He strolled along State Street past places to buy jewelry, ladies' hats, harnesses, and tinware. Near the bakery he sniffed the air—the yeasty aroma of bread reminded him of home.

Remembering how fast the bread had disappeared at breakfast, he strode inside to stock up. The girl behind the counter wrapped five loaves in paper. "That will be twenty cents." He gave her four nickels and added the bread to his sack.

DONG, DONG! Church bells tolled. *CLANG, CLANG!* The fire bell sounded.

"What's happening?" Gilbert grabbed his gunnysack and ran out the door with the other customers. He looked up and down the street and saw crowds of people hurrying toward Main Street, so he ran that way, too. Shopkeepers locked their doors, putting closed signs out as Gilbert raced past. The fire company rumbled past with their hook and ladder wagon.

Rounding the corner of Main Street, he saw throngs of people bunched around the front of Corbin's Saloon. President Thompson, flanked by all the men who had been with him yesterday, stood like a stone wall in the center of a crowd of citizens.

Gilbert slipped into the back of the noisy crowd so he could watch without being noticed. He hoped the Corbins would stay inside so they wouldn't see him. Gilbert overheard one man say, "Corbin won't get away with this." People crowded from all directions until hundreds of them filled the narrow street in front of the saloon. Gilbert's jaw dropped when he spotted Freddie.

Freddie stood near the front of the crowd and chanted, "Corbin Saloon. Close up soon!" Soon others in the crowd took up the chant, louder. The fire bell continued to clang, and the church bells tolled.

The crowd grew quiet when Mr. Corbin lurched from the doorway. "Stay back if you value your life!" He brandished two pistols and spouted curses. "I'm ready for you! I'll shoot anyone who attacks me, my wife, or my saloon."

Gilbert gasped. Mr. Corbin threatened to shoot these folks, but they weren't doing anything violent.

President Thompson raised a hand and shouted above the bells. "Please put those pistols away. We're here on a peaceful mission—our weapons are prayer, God's Word, hymns, and speeches."

A man sang the first line of a hymn in a melodious tenor voice. "God's Free Mercy Streameth . . . " The audience joined the next line.

"Over all the world,
And His banner gleameth, by His church unfurled;
Broad and deep and glorious,
As the heaven above,
Shines in might victorious,
His eternal love."

Choosing Sides

Mr. Corbin's face turned redder with each verse the crowd sang. Waving his pistols and muttering curses, he glared at the crowd.

When the last word of the hymn faded away, Corbin shook his gun at President Thompson and the others. "Listen to me, you—" His words were drowned out when Freddie led the crowd in chants again.

During a pause in the chanting, Mr. Corbin shouted. "You declare you are here in peace, yet you or your hired men vandalized my saloon! Overnight vandals broke into my saloon and emptied out my spirits. I demand repayment."

Gilbert's heart pounded. Someone had found a way—an illegal way—to keep Mr. Corbin from opening his saloon.

A tall, bearded man stood on a pile of stones and said, "We did not pour out your alcohol, nor pay anyone else to do it. We didn't even suggest it." The other men around him nodded.

Another man, who looked like a preacher said, "All of us condemn this vandalism."

Mr. Corbin cocked his revolver and pointed it at the preacher. "You're all liars. You're the ones behind all this. I'll sue every one of you to get my money back."

The chants began again. Mrs. Corbin stepped forward and demanded a chance to speak. The crowd quieted when she climbed on the pile of stones, a makeshift pulpit. "The folks in this town try to make rules for everyone else to follow. The vandals who poured out our spirits despise the rights of property. We are law-abiding citizens and have come to Westerville to operate a lawful business."

Gilbert felt a twinge of pity. The Corbins wouldn't be able to open now, with nothing to sell. He thought of his Aunt Ruby marching past saloons and praying. She and the others closed saloons, too, but without breaking the law. It was hard to decide which side he was on.

Mrs. Corbin waved her sunbonnet, including the whole crowd. "You are tormenting my husband. He's a good man, standing by me in sickness and trials. For many years he nursed me while I was blind, till my sight was restored." She climbed down and went back inside.

The crowd murmured in sympathy, and Mr. Corbin lowered his pistols.

A pastor near the front raised his hand over the crowd, who fell silent to hear what he would say. "Let us pray. Oh, Lord, we are a sinful people coming to ask your help when we don't know what to do. Help us protect our young people from the dangers of this evil world, especially the danger of addiction to alcohol. We pray you will work in the heart of Harry Corbin and his wife so they will change to another line of business. We pray for our town to remain a safe haven, free from the sorrow that comes to a family when the father drinks himself into a stupor and beats his wife and children. A town where children do not go hungry because the family breadwinner has spent his earnings on spirits. Please, Lord, help Harry Corbin and his wife make the right decision about what they are about to do. We ask this in the name of our Saviour, Jesus Christ. Amen."

Mr. Corbin opened his mouth to speak, but his voice was drowned out when the tall, bearded man began a hymn, and the crowd joined in.

"Rejoice, the Lord is King!
Your Lord and King adore,
Mortals, give thanks, and sing,
And triumph evermore;
Lift up your heart, lift up your voice,
Rejoice, again I say, rejoice."

Gilbert found himself humming this hymn, one of his favorites. The crowd sang the third verse with enthusiasm.

"His kingdom cannot fail,

He rules o'er earth and heaven;
The keys of death and hell
Are to our Jesus given:
Lift up your heart, lift up your voice,
Rejoice, again I say, rejoice."

Mr. Corbin shouted, "My saloon will serve only pure and wholesome liquors. The state of Ohio allows citizens to apply for a license to sell beer, wine, and ale. I am within my rights to open this saloon."

A young man yelled, "Listen to the mayor."

A portly man in a suit stepped forward and said, "Our village of Westerville, incorporated in 1858, has always been a dry town. Our trustees passed a law prohibiting the sale of spirituous liquors, one of the earliest such laws in the whole state." He turned to Mr. Corbin. "So even if the state of Ohio allows you to sell your wares, you may not sell them in Westerville."

Mr. Corbin took a deep breath, as if to gather strength for this verbal battle. "I challenge this law. I know for a fact Westerville has no right to forbid something the state allows."

Mrs. Corbin slipped out the front door and whispered in her husband's ear. Mr. Corbin made an announcement to the crowd. "Despite your evil efforts, our saloon will open for business right now. We have replaced the beer you vandalized. We have free pretzels, and sandwiches for sale for a nickel."

The Corbins turned to go inside. Two eggs sailed through the air. They missed the Corbins and splattered against the door. Mrs. Corbin screamed, and Mr. Corbin turned and cursed the jeering crowd.

Freddie led chants of "Corbin Saloon. Close up soon!" Soon a different chant of "No beer here! No beer here!" roared out from the crowd.

Mrs. Corbin wiped the spatters of egg from her face. Rotten egg stench turned Gilbert's stomach. What would happen next? A lady on the stone pile raised her hand to get the crowd's attention for her speech. Gilbert couldn't stand to watch any longer. He slung the sack of groceries over his shoulder and trudged toward West Street, the sounds of chanting and singing following him.

12
Another New Job

Gilbert arrived at the house on West Street with a heavy heart as well as a heavy sack of groceries. He replayed the scene of rotten eggs arching through the air and splattering Mr. and Mrs. Corbin. He heard again the stream of curses coming from Mr. Corbin's mouth and the chants led by Freddie, "No beer here!" and "Corbin Saloon, close up soon!" He was amazed at the overwhelming opposition to the Corbin Saloon by the crowd of citizens.

Shadow greeted him at the door, rubbing against his leg. "Hi, Shadow. You're just like Pilot, always glad to see me." The ache of missing his dog grew to include Pa, Annie, and home.

Inside, he unpacked all the groceries from the gunnysack and arranged them on the sideboard. The challenge of firing up the cook-stove occupied his thoughts next. He chuckled as he collected fuel from the front entry. He knew why his housemates hoarded scrap lumber and old newspapers. When the fire crackled in the stove, he hunted for a pot large enough for the roast. He found it under a pile of dirty dishes in the sink and scrubbed it clean.

With the meat simmering on the stove, Gilbert took time for lunch. The problems of his life flooded into his mind at the same time. He wrestled with the fact his family's temperance beliefs clashed with his assistance of the Corbins.

He needed another job, but who would hire him? He knew how to do farm work, and there were farms beyond Alum Creek. He stoked the fire again so the meat would keep cooking and hiked out Main Street and across Alum Creek.

At the first farm, he knocked on the farmhouse door and waited a long time. Nobody came, so he went around back to the garden. A scarecrow guarded the corn patch and a woman and her two young children hoed the rows. Gilbert asked her if she needed help.

The woman chortled. "Every woman needs help keeping ahead of the weeds. But we can't afford to pay. Come back at harvest time when my husband hires extra field hands." Gilbert's shoulder's drooped. He hoped to be going to school in the fall, not harvesting corn. But who would help Pa harvest corn? He ignored the guilt pang.

Gilbert thanked her and hiked toward the next farm. There, two fierce-looking dogs chased him away in full view of the farmer. Gilbert decided that was another "no" answer. He turned back, retracing his steps to try farms at the other end of the road.

The next farm impressed Gilbert with its large barn, many outbuildings, and fields of corn. A bearded man driving a team pulling a wagonload of clay clopped past, so Gilbert followed. The wagon stopped in front of a lean-to with clay tiles stacked to dry. The man had an air of authority so Gilbert guessed he would be the one to ask about a job.

"Hello, sir, is this your farm?"

"Yep. I'm John Everal. What can I do for you today, sonny?"

"My name's Gilbert Freeman, and I'm looking for a summer job."

Mr. Everal took off his hat, showing a white forehead above a tanned face. He combed his hair with his fingers, took the measure of the young man before him, and put his hat back on.

Gilbert guessed he should speak up about his skills. "I've done hard work, so I'm stronger than I look."

"I can take you for a trial period." Mr. Everal nodded toward a long, low building. "My tile factory has a big order, and I could use you in the mornings. I can pay you seventy-five cents for a half day, starting at seven. The missus even feeds us a midday meal. How soon can you start?"

"Tomorrow, sir."

Gilbert whistled all the way back from the Everals. He looked forward to this new job and the wages he'd earn. The ugly scenes of the morning receded to the back of his mind.

In the kitchen, he added fuel to the stove, inhaling the delicious roast pork smell. Gilbert chuckled at Shadow—he also smelled supper cooking and perched on a chair to watch. "You're the mouser, Shadow. You must catch your own supper."

He counted out potatoes, carrots, and onions and peeled them, glad for his few cooking skills. The pot still had space after he had added them all, so he dropped in two more potatoes and three more carrots, nibbling the last one to make it fit.

Gilbert cleared off the clutter from the table in the dining room. Vern arrived and offered to set the table. The others arrived and crowded into the kitchen, cheering when they peeked into the pot.

Gilbert crossed his arms. "Every time you lift the lid, it slows down the cooking."

Freddie sliced a loaf of bread and Gilbert carried the enormous pot of meat and vegetables to the table.

The three housemates watched and salivated as Gilbert lined up four plates. "I'm doing my best to divide everything equally."

Vern raised his hand. "Since I set the table, you should give me the biggest helping."

Benjie said, "Whoa. I'm the hungriest, so I need more than you all."

"Quiet!" Freddie said. "You're slowing Gilbert down, and I want to get my teeth into this grub."

Gilbert handed each one a plateful, and they set to work. He remembered with a twinge of guilt that Pa always prayed before meals.

"You sure can cook," Freddie said.

Vern waved a forkful of meat. "Too bad there won't be seconds. By the way, did everyone see the fireworks when the Corbins opened their saloon?"

Freddie said, "I told you it was coming."

Gilbert stared at Freddie. "Yes, I saw the crowd, and I heard you adding to the noise with your chants. You and the mob were rude to the Corbins."

Freddie took a large bite. "They got what they deserved. They knew Westerville was dead set against a saloon. How long has this town been dry, anyway?"

Benjie liked to be the one with facts and figures. "According to Mayor Clark's speech, the town passed an ordinance when they incorporated in 1858, so they've been dry seventeen years."

"But somebody dumped out all their beer and whiskey. That's vandalism!" A lump rose in Gilbert's throat.

Vern chimed in on Gilbert's side. "The Corbins got a raw deal from Westerville."

Freddie shook his head. "What bothered me the most about that pair—they were deaf to what everyone told them. I counted a dozen people or more, even women, who gave speeches. Every last one of the speeches said the same thing. 'We do not want a saloon in our town.'"

Freddie gave Gilbert a pointed stare. "You said the mob was rude to the Corbins. Did you hear the curses and ugly language Corbin used? He even called Bishop Hanby a silver-topped . . . well, I won't repeat his insult to that honorable man."

Gilbert concentrated on eating his supper, which didn't taste so good anymore. He wanted to defend the Corbins, but he had to agree with Freddie about Mr. Corbin's foul language.

Freddie kept the conversation going. "They say Ohio law allows them to sell alcohol. But does that make it the right thing to do?" He answered his own question. "No, it's not the right thing to do." Freddie paused and spoke in a low tone. "Gil, here's why I joined the crowd against Corbin's saloon. How would you feel if your father came home drunk every Friday night and beat your mother? That happened all the time to me and my younger sisters. Us kids would always hide, but there were times we'd get beaten, too. Often my mother had no money to feed us, and we went hungry. Neighbors took pity on us, even offering a safe place to hide from Pa."

Gilbert's heart twisted in sympathy for Freddie. He had never heard anyone talk about living in fear because his pa was a drunk. He looked at his new friend and shook his head. "I'd feel terrible if that was my family. I get it why you're dead set against the Corbins opening a saloon."

Vern shook his head. "If the temperance people didn't try to make the rules for everyone else, they'd have a stronger case." He stood and stacked the plates, holding up one with a laugh. "This one looks like it's been licked clean."

Freddie said, "Gil, we all really appreciate you fixing supper tonight."

Vern stuck his head in from the kitchen. "Yeah, I was getting tired of beans."

"That was the best meal I've had since I left home," Benjie said. "Gil, will you be able to top it tomorrow night?"

"Maybe. Today I got a half-day factory job at Everal Tile."

Benjie's look showed he couldn't believe it. "You must have an honest face. You get hired right off the bat."

"I'll pump water and set it to heating," Freddie said as he carried out the empty pot. Everybody clean up his own stuff, and then we can get a card game going."

Gilbert washed his own plate last, after scraping bits of meat on the floor for Shadow. He could hear his housemates joking as they played their card game. He stuck his head in the dining room. “Night, fellas, I’m calling it a day.”

Gilbert dragged himself up the steps and slumped on the bed, sure he would fall asleep right away. Instead, the dreadful scenes of the morning replayed in his mind. He wished the whole Corbin thing had never happened.

13
Gilbert the Cart Man

The sun was already up, so Gilbert dressed quickly. He didn't want to be late for his first day of work. He hoped his housemates wouldn't say a word about Corbin—last night made him question which side he was on.

Freddie acted as if there had been no intense discussion the night before. "Come join us for breakfast. We've already sliced the bread, and here's the jam."

"Thanks." Gilbert grabbed two slices and slathered them with raspberry jam. "I'll eat them while I walk to work."

Even though it was two blocks in the wrong direction, Gilbert zipped past the Corbin Saloon to see if it had any scars from the awful scene the day before. He gaped at the damage. In front of every window, shards of glass glittered in the morning sun. He wondered who did it and when. He left, glad he wasn't still working for the Corbins.

When Gilbert arrived at the Everal tile factory, Mr. Everal showed him around and introduced him to three workers. They nodded and smiled at Gilbert. Mr. Everal nodded toward a fourth man working in a corner. "Jasper there operates the machine that rolls the tiles from the clay, and then he puts them on a cart. Once he has a cart full, your job is to move the tiles to the drying shed behind the building. You'll unload it onto the drying racks."

"I can do that."

Mr. Everal led Gilbert to Jasper's side. "This is Gilbert. He's your cart man today." Jasper scowled and turned back to operating his machine. Gilbert had a sinking feeling that Jasper would be a tough boss.

Since the first cart was already stacked with tiles, Gilbert got right to work. He tugged the cart, grunting, till it rolled toward the door. Once in the shed, he unloaded the tiles, and hurried back with the empty cart. Sweat dripped from his face—not only due to the heat but also because he worried he'd make a mistake.

When he returned to the tile-rolling machine, Jasper had already loaded the second cart. "I knew when the boss brought you in you couldn't keep up." He stacked tiles on a third cart.

Gilbert's face reddened, and he searched for a good excuse. "That cart's too heavy to pull fast."

"It's your job. Speed it up."

Gilbert worked faster at unloading, but he discovered that hurrying made things worse. When he transferred the last layer of tiles, he knocked the edge of the pile. Five tiles tumbled to the ground and broke. Gilbert hurried back, but not fast enough for Jasper. Anger and discouragement made Gilbert think the morning would never end.

All factory work stopped when Mrs. Everal rang the dinner bell. Gilbert followed Mr. Everal and the four tile workers inside to a long table already loaded with food.

Mrs. Everal tied napkins around the necks of her two boys, ages seven and two, who sat at the far end of the table. Gilbert asked their names.

"I'm Alvin. I'm going to make tiles, like Papa."

"Frankie be like Papa, too."

Mr. Everal asked the blessing and grabbed the top plate from the stack in front of him. He dished out generous helpings of mashed potatoes, gravy, sliced pork, applesauce, and turnips. The only sounds were the clank of silverware against the plates and the sound of food being chewed. Frankie and Alvin concentrated on eating.

Gilbert watched Jasper. He was a big man and enjoyed eating, but the tasty meal hadn't removed the scowl from his face.

At the end of the meal, Gilbert thanked Mrs. Everal. "Your cooking reminds me of home—it's delicious."

"I've saved the best till last." She nodded toward the two cherry pies on the counter. "Would you please bring them over, with that knife beside them?"

The four other workmen devoured their slices and asked for seconds. Gilbert wished for more but thought he shouldn't ask. Mrs. Everal glanced his way and slid the pie plate down to him. "Gilbert, this last piece has your name on it."

He studied the crust, a lattice crust like his mother used to make. Before he could take a bite, he had to wait for the lump in his throat to go away.

Mr. Everal handed him three quarters. "See you tomorrow at seven."

"Yes, sir. Thank you, sir."

When the workers filed out to return to work, Jasper grimaced at Gilbert.

Gilbert stopped at the house to get his gunnysack and hiked toward town to shop for supper, right past the Corbin Saloon. Two workmen replaced the broken windows. Inside he saw both Corbins and several customers. He wanted to say hello but he feared the Corbins might get in trouble, since he was underage.

Gilbert headed to the butcher first. Ahead, a young lady wearing a stylish hat grabbed his attention. When she turned to go into Redding and Clark's Grocery, he recognized her. "Rose—are you shopping, too?"

She lifted her basket. "I'm getting things for supper."

"Me, too." Gilbert showed his gunnysack. "I'm the official cook for my three housemates."

"Let's shop together." She raised her eyebrows, and Gilbert noticed how blue her eyes were.

Gilbert held the door for her. "You can give me advice. I'm new at this."

"Let me see your list."

Gilbert reddened. "I don't have one. I just walk around and look. By the way, did you see the damage to the Corbin place?"

"No. What happened?"

"Somebody busted their windows."

"Do they know who did it?" Elizabeth asked.

"No." Gilbert stopped in front of the barrel of flour. Rose nodded to the clerk, who weighed out five pounds for her.

"Do you need flour, too? Rose asked.

Gilbert shook his head. "I don't know how to bake anything." He returned to the topic. "Westerville is getting a bad reputation from the things done to that saloon."

Rose put the flour in her basket and nodded. "The preachers speak out against the vandalism at the mass temperance meetings."

Gilbert rubbed his chin. "What meetings?"

Rose walked further down the aisle. "All the churches are taking turns having mass meetings to rally the town against the saloon. Of course, our family has been to the two they've had so far. You should come with us."

"Maybe I will." He guessed he'd hear the other side of the story there.

Rose pointed to a large handbill in the bakery window. "Look at that. I've seen them in both stores where I've shopped."

Gilbert read it aloud. "We, the undersigned citizens of Westerville and vicinity, hereby solemnly pledge ourselves that we will not patronize any dry goods merchant, groceryman, physician, lawyer, mechanic, or any other business man, or employ for any purpose a laboring man, or hire help that will frequent, encourage, sustain, or furnish aid to a liquor saloon in Westerville." He shook his head. "That includes everybody in town."

"It has hundreds of signatures on it." Rose bent close to read the rest. "Papa's is there, too. Papa said something about a pledge passed around by a committee he's on. A vigilance committee, now I remember."

Gilbert said, "That will make life tough for the Corbins. Everyone who has signed that pledge promises not to sell them anything."

"It's a fair way to fight the saloon, not like the vandalizers do." Rose stopped in front of a display and placed a bottle of vinegar in her basket.

Gilbert looked at the display and shook his head. "What's vinegar good for?"

Rose hid a giggle behind her hand. "Too many things to tell you about in a short time."

Gilbert chuckled. "I have a lot to learn. That reminds me—are you going to school this fall?"

"Yes, Papa wants his girls to be educated. I'm enrolled in Otterbein Academy."

Gilbert couldn't suppress a smile. Rose had given him another reason to want to go to school in the fall. "I'd like to be one of your classmates."

Rose's eyes sparkled. "That would be outstanding."

When their shopping was complete, Gilbert didn't want the conversation to end. "May I carry your heavy basket home for you?"

Rose blushed and handed him the basket. The two-blocks to the corner of Grove and Home Streets ended too soon for Gilbert. He stayed and chatted with her on the front porch swing.

Rose stood and glanced at the front door. "I'd better get inside to help Mama. You always have an invitation at our house for Sunday dinner."

"Maybe I'll take you up on that some Sunday."

"Thank you for carrying my market-basket home." She turned to go inside but paused at the door to wave.

Gilbert shouldered his groceries and floated back to West Street with a light heart.

He worked to get supper, but everywhere he moved around the kitchen, Shadow arrived first and rubbed his leg. He kindled a fire in the stove, and the pot of potatoes was simmering when Freddie arrived.

"What's for supper?"

"So far, potatoes. But I have green beans and ham to go with them."

After Freddie set the table, he sprawled in his favorite chair to read the newspaper. "I wonder if Corbin and his saloon will be in the news today."

Gilbert sliced the ham into a skillet and set it on to fry. "Someone broke all the windows. It's a mess. Corbin will go out of business." He snapped the beans and put them on to cook.

"But he's fighting back. Here's the headline: 'Seven Face Judge Remmy.'" Freddie read a few more lines but was interrupted by the arrival of the others. Everyone crowded into the kitchen to see what was cooking for supper.

After the four young men had filled their plates, the conversation buzzed with all the details of what Corbin had done.

Freddie read aloud about the arraignment of the seven citizens before the magistrate in Columbus. He slapped the paper down. "The only crime those seven men are guilty of is standing up for what's right. There's no way any of them took part in the vandalism against Corbin's Saloon."

Vern said, "Then they'll be found innocent, of course."

Freddie waved the newspaper. "Maybe not. This article says Judge Remmy supports the right of saloons to sell beer."

Vern asked, "Even when the town has a regulation on the books against it?"

Freddie put his finger on the paper. "Yep, it says so."

Gilbert had less sympathy for the Corbins because they dragged seven upstanding citizens into court. Even so, he countered with the other side of the argument. "But this arraignment was the only way Corbin had to fight back against the vandalism."

Freddie leaned close to Gilbert's face. "He doesn't have to fight—he could close the saloon. The vandalism would stop if he opened another sort of business."

Gilbert bit his lip. "We should try to look at both sides of the question."

Freddie shook his head. "Corbin's on the wrong side, no two ways about it." He carried his plate to the kitchen. Shadow bounded to follow him, hoping for scraps. "I'll pump the water and set it on to heat."

Vern plopped the pots in the sink and complimented Gilbert on another great meal. "We're lucky to have you, you're such a good cook."

The approval of his housemates warmed Gilbert's heart. It made him think about home. He wondered if Pa was able to do the chores without his help. He wondered how Annie was doing at Aunt Ruby's. He wondered if he'd ever go home again.

Benjie joined them in the kitchen. "Tonight's a full moon—a good night to go out for pranks. Want to come, Gil?"

"What sort of pranks?" Gilbert remembered their tales of past escapades. He didn't want to get into trouble.

Vern lowered his voice. "We could stake out Corbin's Saloon and maybe catch the vandals."

"I doubt we'll catch them, but why not try?" Gilbert liked the idea.

Vern, Benjie, and Gilbert dressed in dark clothes and walked through back alleys at dusk. Dogs barked and crickets chirped as the boys crept toward Main Street. Gilbert shivered with anticipation—what might happen? They hunched against the shed behind the Corbin saloon and spied Mr. Corbin locking the door and disappearing into the dark.

"Looks like he got the windows replaced," Gilbert said.

"Ssh! Did you hear that?" Benjie craned his neck toward a rustling noise behind them.

"Stay in the shadows," Gilbert whispered. He held his breath and the rustling came closer. "Oh!" Gilbert jumped as two scrawny dogs ran past them toward Main Street.

Vern snickered. "We get to know the local mutts when we're out on pranks."

"Maybe Corbin should get a watchdog," Gil said.

"Good idea," said Benjie. "Maybe you should stop by and suggest it."

"You're joking? I'm not allowed in a saloon, am I?"

Vern said, "They're not allowed to serve you alcohol, but there's no law against you being there. Except maybe your Pa's rule."

Gilbert sighed. Pa would rake him over the coals if he went into a saloon. But Pa would never find out. Gilbert decided he would visit Mr. Corbin soon.

The three of them watched for vandals for a few hours. Two men walked past on the sidewalk, joking and laughing. A raccoon slipped through the shadows on its way to visit the Corbin garbage bin. Two or three cats in a nearby alley screeched for ten minutes until someone shouted from a window and threw a heavy object at them.

Gilbert decided it wasn't as exciting as he had imagined. "Nothing happening."

"So, let's call it a night." Benjie turned toward West Street.

"But now Gil knows the ropes," Vern said. "Next time, we'll capture the criminal."

Gilbert grinned. "You bet. Detective Freeman always catches his man."

As they headed home, Vern grabbed Gilbert's cap, and Benjie mussed his hair.

14
Temperance Meeting

Gilbert stopped inside the door of the Everal Tile Factory. Jasper would arrive soon, so he could relax until then.

The other workers raised their voices to carry over the clatter. One man said, "Have any of you seen a tall fellow around town—a stranger?"

Another replied, "Yes, I've seen him twice near Corbin's. Isn't he under suspicion for the vandalism?"

"I think so. Did you hear the latest about the Corbin Saloon?" a third man asked.

"Sure did. Somebody raised the roof. Bet they used strong explosives."

The first worker said, "I heard this from a buddy . . . a small figure of a man carved from wood got left in plain sight by whoever did the deed."

Gilbert's brow furrowed as he listened to the gossip about the explosion at Corbin's Saloon.

Jasper's voice boomed from across the room. "Gilbert, quit lazing around. What a slowpoke. Everal expects you to keep up with me."

Gilbert pulled the empty cart toward Jasper, who scowled as he transferred tiles to fill it. "Take it away—and don't take forever to bring it back."

As Gilbert towed the cart, Jasper ranted about Corbin to the other workers. "Corbin got what he had coming to him. Don't be surprised when you hear something worse happens. In fact, I hope somebody blows the roof all the way off."

Gilbert wondered if Jasper could be planning to be that somebody. He leaned his weight into hauling the full cart toward the drying shed. He tried to keep track of how many trips he made—this helped the morning to pass more quickly.

At quitting time, Mr. Everal loped to his side. "How are things going, Gilbert?"

"Same as usual—Jasper tells me I work too slow. But if I go faster, I break tiles."

Mr. Everal pushed back his hat. "Jasper is a fast worker, and I'd hoped you could keep up. Be more careful—I don't like to hear about broken tiles."

"I'll keep trying." Gilbert hesitated, wondering if he should mention what he had heard from Jasper. "Jasper said he hoped somebody would blow Corbin's roof off."

"From Jasper, it's hot air. But keep your ears open and report back."

Gilbert nodded, but he thought Mr. Everal was too trusting.

"Here's your pay for the day. After you return the empty cart, stop by to see the missus. Instead of a noon meal today, she has food toward your supper."

Gilbert peeked into the kitchen of the Everal farmstead. Alvin zoomed a wooden wagon across the floor to knock down Frankie's wall. Mrs. Everal wielded a paring knife over a pile of potatoes. When she saw Gilbert, she nodded toward a small bucket. "Can you use two dozen eggs? They're cracked so they must be used right away." She dropped her voice. "Alvin tripped when he collected them this morning."

"Thanks. We'll put them on the menu." He mussed Frankie's hair and headed home with the bucket.

– Choosing Sides –

Gilbert walked past the Corbin saloon to see the damage they'd talked about at the tile factory. The roof had been lifted several inches, and the glass from the windows lay on the sidewalk. He saw Mr. Corbin inside and went in to talk with him.

"Hey, Mr. Corbin. Thought I'd stop by and see how you're doing."

"Oh, I'm gearing up for battle. How are you faring these days?"

"I've got a job at Mr. Everal's tile factory."

Corbin sneered. "Everal is one of the temperance crowd. You see what they've done to my saloon?"

Gilbert looked around at the damage. "Your mirror is cracked—I remember helping you hang it." Gilbert saw something on Mr. Corbin's shelf. "What's that man carved from wood ?"

Corbin walked over to the shelf behind the bar. "The vandals left us a souvenir." He handed a small woodcarving of a man to Gilbert.

"It's in two pieces. That's odd."

Corbin took the figure back. "Criminals in this town are trying to scare us into closing, but it's not working. Mrs. Corbin and I won't give them the pleasure of running us out of town."

Gilbert looked around at the damage. "Have you thought of getting a watchdog to protect your property? We have a good dog at the farm. He keeps the varmints out of the henhouse."

"If I had the chance, I'd take a shotgun to those worthless vermin." Mr. Corbin pretended he was loading a gun and shooting the invisible enemies. Gilbert thought he would not like to be in Mr. Corbin's line of fire.

Mr. Corbin pulled at his beard. "But a snarling watchdog—you may have something there."

Gilbert grabbed his bucket of eggs. "I hope you can catch the guilty ones."

After supper, Freddie sprang an idea on Gilbert. "You said we should look at both sides of the temperance question. Come along with me to the mass temperance meeting tonight."

Gilbert wasn't too hard to convince, since he knew Rose Goodspeed would be there. He and Freddie hiked the few blocks to Otterbein's Administration Building and followed the crowd to the chapel.

The atmosphere felt electric as many in the crowd called out greetings to one another. Gilbert looked for Rose and her family but didn't see them in the crowd. This meeting might not be boring, as the Goodspeed girls had described the meetings they'd attended. All around him families filed into the pews. It looked as if the whole town had turned out against the Corbins. The temperance people were in the majority—maybe they were right.

He spotted the Everal family and waved to them and pulled Freddie's arm. "Let's sit with my friends, the Everals." As soon as they slid into the pew, Frankie and Alvin elbowed their way to sit on each side of Gilbert.

A short man with a salt-and-pepper beard stepped to the front. "Let's all stand and sing the Temperance Battle Hymn. You know the tune, now sing it out."

Gilbert did know the tune, since he'd often sung The Battle Hymn of the Republic, but he hadn't heard these words before. Everyone around him sang the song by heart.

Gilbert smiled as the Everal boys shouted the chorus. "Glory, glory, hallelujah, Glory, glory, hallelujah, Glory, glory, hallelujah, As we go marching on."

He chuckled to himself over the words of the third verse—they did not sound like what was happening in Westerville.

"We wield no carnal weapons,
And we hurl no fiery dart,
But with words of love and reason,
We are sure to win the heart,

And persuade the poor transgressor
To prefer the better part.
Our God is marching on."

A pink-cheeked man mounted the steps to the pulpit. Mr. Everal whispered to Gilbert, "That's Reverend Wallace. He has a real heart for his flock."

The preacher read from a huge pulpit Bible. "Think not that I am come to send peace on earth: I came not to send peace, but a sword." He waved an imaginary sword over the crowd. "A sword! A weapon that cuts and divides. Jesus knew families would be divided over his words."

Gilbert nodded—this town—his family, too, was divided. His father and Aunt Ruby would be shocked if they discovered he had worked for the Corbins. Gilbert still had a little sympathy for the embattled couple. Maybe tonight he'd learn what motivated the town to fight Corbin so hard.

As the sermon continued, Gilbert spotted the Goodspeed sisters sitting beside their parents. Rose turned and caught his eye and they traded smiles. He mused over the fact that Rose and Iva were at this temperance meeting and probably wishing they were at home, yet he had run away from home and now sat in a temperance meeting. He did not like being the one who divided his family, but he'd never be a temperance crusader like Pa and Aunt Ruby.

15
The Unseen Witness

One morning when Gilbert reported for work, Mr. Everal sent him to the house. "My wife needs a garden helper right now more than I need a tile worker. You'll get the same pay for your half-day, but it's much easier work."

He knocked on the door and inhaled the sweet perfume of the roses growing on a trellis beside the porch. Mrs. Everal called out, "Come in, come in, Gilbert." The breakfast smells—ham, eggs, pancakes—made his mouth water.

She stood at the sink washing the breakfast dishes, pots, and pans. "Gilbert, have you had breakfast?" The two Everal boys stopped stacking blocks in a tower and ran over to hug him.

Gilbert nodded. "Yes, Ma'am, but I guess by the wonderful smells it wasn't as delicious as the one you served."

"Maybe we'll include breakfast as part of your pay. Sit down—I'll get you some ham. Boys, Gilbert's going to help with our garden."

Alvin grinned up at the tall boy in front of him. "Can you dig holes?"

Mrs. Everal had a question for him, too. "Have you had experience gardening? Can you tell a weed from a plant?"

"Yes, I used to help my mother every summer."

"What's your last name? Maybe I know your family."

"Freeman. We live about six miles north of Westerville, in Genoa Township."

"Yes, I met your mother several years ago at a church social. We were saddened to hear of her passing."

Gilbert blinked back a sudden tear. The pain of his mother's death was still fresh, and his guilt made it worse. "She always had a big garden."

"Here's bread and butter to go with the ham." Mrs. Everal went back to washing dishes.

Under the watchful eyes of Albert and Frankie, Gilbert wolfed down his second breakfast.

Mrs. Everal got out the butter churn and poured it halfway full of cream. "The tool shed is out back beside the garden. Hoe the weeds in the sweet corn rows. I'll be out when this butter comes."

"Yes, Ma'am." Gilbert plopped his hat on his head and hurried to the task. Chopping weeds from between the corn rows helped him work out his frustration over all that had happened to the Corbins. The vandalism would surely put them out of business.

Mrs. Everal and her boys strolled out to the garden. The boys chased each other and their collie dog while Mrs. Everal helped hoe the rows of corn. Next she knelt beside the rows of carrots. "These seedlings are too crowded. Unless we pull at least half of them out, the others can't grow large."

Gilbert selected six tiny carrots and pulled them up. Mrs. Everal demonstrated her method, which was much faster. "Be ruthless. We'll feed the thinnings to the chickens. You might even find one big enough to eat."

Working beside the efficient Mrs. Everal, Gilbert learned new ways to do many garden chores. As they worked, they chatted.

When Gilbert mentioned the Corbin Saloon, Mrs. Everal clucked her tongue. "I've been following that story in the paper. The whole town has battled the Corbin Saloon from opening day."

Gilbert tossed his handful of weeds toward the growing pile beside the garden. "People are breaking the law."

"Vandals give upright townspeople a black eye, since it looks like the town leaders dumped the liquor, broke the windows, and exploded the gunpowder."

"Westerville's reaction doesn't match the problem. They've made alcohol a giant enemy. Is a saloon really that bad?"

Mrs. Everal stood and gazed into the distance. "You're right to think they've gone overboard, but . . . " She trailed off. She rubbed the middle of her back. "Pick up the pile of weeds and come with me to the compost pile. I want to show you something."

The boys marched behind their mother and Gilbert—they didn't want to miss whatever it was. Mrs. Everal pulled up a long piece of an attractive, white-flowering vine climbing above the piles of worn out plants and weeds. "This is morning glory bindweed. Look at its pretty flower and heart-shaped leaf. Don't let the good looks fool you—it's impossible to get rid of the pesky thing! It has deep roots, so the best thing to do is never let it get started."

Gilbert noticed the bindweed had grown throughout the whole area around the compost pile. "Oh, I get it. Because, like the bindweed, drinking looks pleasing at first, but once it gets started . . . "

"Right. Let liquor get a hold on your life, and it won't let go. We'll have to plow this area deeply this fall, rake up the bindweed roots and burn them." She chuckled. "And then we're careful about where we put the ashes."

Gilbert's gardening days began with early-morning freshness, but by mid-morning, he dripped with sweat. On the third day, his work did not go well. He accidentally hoed down a row of seedlings, thinking they were weeds. A painful blister appeared on the palm of his hand from hoeing. He shouted at Frankie to stop throwing clods of dirt at Alvin, so Frankie went crying to his mother, telling her how mean Gilbert had been to him.

At noon, Mrs. Everal said nothing about Frankie's story, but instead handed Gilbert a brown paper package. "Sausage for your supper tonight. We butchered a pig for a family reunion, and this is extra."

"Thank you! My housemates will thank you, too. How should I fix it?"

"Brown it first and keep it warm on a platter. Then slice potatoes and onions in the skillet. Lots of salt and pepper, too."

"Thanks much, Mrs. Everal. See you tomorrow morning."

Gilbert headed home to fix supper. He needed to succeed at this cook's job since it earned him free room and board.

After he had the stove going and the sausage frying, Freddie burst into the room. "Sausage! Do I smell sausage?"

"Yep. I'm getting ready to fry potatoes next. You're here in time to set the table."

Freddie stacked the plates and silverware together and headed into the dining room. "You hear the news about Corbin?"

Gilbert jerked to attention. "No. What happened?"

"He was arrested and jailed. They booked him for assault with intent to kill."

"Whoa! I'm not surprised." Gilbert shook his head. "I couldn't stand watching him point those pistols at the crowd."

"Even though he's in jail, the saloon is still open. I went past after work today, and this barefooted guy was sitting on the bar, and Mrs. Corbin was talking to customers. The fellows buying drinks might be from out of town—I didn't recognize them. Lots of Westervillans are teetotalers."

While they sat around enjoying the sausage and potatoes, Gilbert learned more details about Corbin. Freddie said, "When Corbin paid his bond and got out of jail on the first warrant, Westerville was ready with two or three other charges."

Vern waved a copy of The Columbus Daily Evening Dispatch. "The newspaper calls this whole thing Westerville's Whiskey War. They say the preachers encourage vandalism at the mass meetings."

"I believe that." Benjie wagged his finger at the others. "They probably preach the Corbin Saloon is so evil that somebody should help God do away with it."

Gilbert shook his head. "I was at a temperance meeting, and I didn't hear anything like that."

Later, Gilbert lay awake, thinking about Corbin in jail, wondering about his Pa, tossing and turning in bed. The neighbors slammed their front door, as they did every night at bedtime. The light rain had stopped, the moon cast eerie shadows, and every little noise floated through the still air. The neighbor's dog barked at a trespasser. Gilbert looked out the window and spotted two figures as they raced around the corner of the house toward the street. The dog stopped barking.

Gilbert added up the clues—those men were headed toward Main Street, and at this time of night, they were up to no good. Maybe they were going to Corbin's. Gilbert jumped into his shoes and raced out the front door. His heart pounded, and he nearly turned back, since it was crazy to think he could catch them.

The moon illuminated West Street. Nobody was in sight, but Gilbert heard dogs barking ahead. The men must be around the corner.

Gilbert turned left on Main Street, toward Corbin's. He saw two figures in the shadows, but when he looked again, they were gone. He crept close to the Corbin Saloon, but stayed in the shadows, afraid the men would jump him.

Gilbert watched and waited for long minutes. Shivering with suspense, he wondered if anything would happen. A small, white object sailed through the air and struck the Corbin Saloon sign. "Splat!" One after another, eggs splatted against the door, the window, and the front of the building, leaving gooey, golden streaks. His stomach lurched when the rotten egg stench wafted toward him.

Gilbert remained frozen in place—he wanted to take action, but he was outnumbered. He determined to follow the pair, to gather as much information as he could against them. The two figures emerged from the shadows and headed back down Main Street. Both were heavy-set, with one larger than the other.

He followed at a distance, keeping in the shadows. The figures continued past West Street, crossed Alum Creek, and turned right on the dirt road that went past the Everals.

The Everal's collie raced toward the figures, barking, and they took off running. Gilbert did too, but he ran back to West Street. He took off his shoes on the front porch and tiptoed to bed.

16
Answers and Questions

Gilbert came downstairs the next morning in time to join Freddie, Vern, and Benjie, sprawled around the parlor. He grabbed two slices of bread and buttered and jammed them. "You're not going to believe what I did last night."

Benjie said, "You went to bed like the rest of us and had a wild dream."

"No, I was wide awake the whole time. I looked out the window and saw two men cut through our yard. I had a hunch they were not out for an evening stroll, so I jumped up and followed them."

Vern said, "No fooling?"

"That could be dangerous," Freddie said. "Where'd they go?"

"They egged Corbin's Saloon."

"Do you know who it was?" Benjie asked.

"I never saw their faces, only their shapes from the back. Both of them were big, the kind who could wrestle me to the ground. That's why I didn't challenge them, but I followed them. They went across Alum Creek. I think they live on the same road as the Everals."

Freddie grinned and took a bite of his jam sandwich. "Those two, whoever they were, did a service for Westerville. Corbin got what he deserved, if you ask me."

Gilbert's face turned red. "But it's against the law to throw rotten eggs at somebody's business."

"They fought Corbin with what he understands." Freddie said. "Westerville failed to get him out with anything they've tried so far—the Vigilance Committee's work, the pledge signed by hundreds of citizens. Or the mass temperance meetings."

"But still, they shouldn't break the law." Benjie fixed himself another piece of bread and butter.

Freddie's voice rose a notch. "You think Corbin is right to open a saloon?"

Vern said, "Not morally right, maybe. But if Ohio Law says he has the right, then they should fight him lawfully."

Gilbert nodded, glad to have someone on his side. "Whoever broke his windows, poured out his beer and whiskey, exploded the gunpowder, tossed the rotten eggs—those vandals should be jailed. They're breaking the law."

Vern stood and motioned to Benjie. "We better get to work."

After the others left, Freddie patted Gilbert on the back. "You guys are brave to stand up for Corbin's rights."

Gilbert crossed his arms. "It's not only Corbin's rights, but everyone's right to live in a town where everyone obeys the law. Otherwise, it's mob rule."

Freddie rubbed his chin. "You've got a good point. I have to agree, even though I'm against Corbin. Westerville should thrash the lawbreakers and bring them to justice."

Gilbert headed out the door to work with Mrs. Everal. The dew sparkled on the grass as she and Gilbert walked toward the garden. She spread her hands toward the neat rows of vegetables. "Gilbert, my garden has never looked this good in July. You've made the difference this year."

Gilbert felt his face redden. "Thank you, Ma'am."

"In fact, I bragged about you to a friend at our Women's Prayer Circle meeting. She begged me to let you come work for her, even for a half day."

Alvin raced from the far side of the garden. "Can I dig a hole beside the sunflowers for a bunny trap?"

"A good idea. Get the small shovel from the shed to dig your hole. And a trowel so Frankie can help." Alvin raced away, and Mrs. Everal continued explaining. "I felt it was selfish to keep you to myself. My friend's husband is Jasper, the man you work beside. Their son Lester has become rebellious. He's their only child—he's 14 years of age. Sylvia is worried about him. We both thought you could be a good example for him."

Gilbert's jaw dropped. "M-me?"

"Of course. You've been a good example for my boys."

Gilbert thought of his rebellion against his father. Mrs. Everal didn't know what he was really like. "I'll try."

Mrs. Everal gestured toward her garden. "Lester will work beside you in the garden, and you'll have a chance to influence him."

Gilbert's mind flooded with questions, but he asked the most important one. "When would this new job begin?"

"Today. Their place is right down the road, so you can walk there in five or ten minutes." She studied Gilbert to make sure the plan was acceptable. "I hope you don't mind. The pay would be the same, and the work also."

Gilbert tilted his head. "I'm glad for the work—the garden work—but I don't know if I can help Lester."

"Do your best. His mother and I will be praying for you—and we've been praying for him for months."

Gilbert waved goodbye to the boys, who were so busy digging they didn't notice, and headed to the Mossman farm. He trudged down the road with doubts spinning in his mind. Maybe he and Lester wouldn't get along. Maybe his work wouldn't be good enough. If that happened, he'd be back at the Everals—that would be fine with him. He smiled and walked a little faster.

The white farmhouse, circled by a picket fence, reminded Gilbert of a picture from a storybook his mother read to him as a child—Old McDonald's Farm. His knock was answered by a plump woman with pink cheeks and a flock of worry creases in her brow. "Gilbert? I'm so glad you came." She called out to her son. "Lester, come meet Gilbert. He's come to help you in the garden."

When Lester didn't appear, the woman grasped Gilbert's hand. "I'm Mrs. Mossman. My husband works for Mr. Everal."

"Pleased to meet you, Ma'am."

"You and Lester can get started right away, while the day is still cool." She led the way through the house. Gilbert noticed shelves filled with wood carvings, especially duck decoys.

"Your husband must be a hunter."

Mrs. Mossman raised her eyebrows. "Why did you think . . . oh, the decoys. No, he just likes carving decoys and other things. You should hear him when he gets going with his mallet and chisel."

Grabbing a sun hat, she led the way out the kitchen door. Lester sat on the back-porch steps. "Oh, there you are, Lester. Come with us to the corn patch. Collect two hoes from the shed on the way." Lester's broad shoulders made Gilbert feel like a string bean in comparison.

Lester clambered as slowly as possible to get the hoes from a whitewashed shed. He gave the newcomer a long stare before thrusting a hoe toward him.

"You can start in the corn rows, boys." She grabbed a basket to fill with green beans.

As Gilbert hoed, he searched for a good conversation-opener. "Looks to be hot today."

Lester grunted and kept hoeing. He worked without energy and missed half the weeds.

Gilbert tried again to start a conversation. "I really like sweet corn. How about you?"

Lester ignored him and kept hoeing.

When they finished the corn, Mrs. Mossman led them to the carrot rows. "Thin these next." Gilbert's spirit lifted. Mrs. Everal had taught him how to thin carrots, so he knelt and pulled the crowded seedlings, leaving the larger ones.

Lester frowned. "What are you doing? Get out of the way. You're doing it all wrong." He pushed Gilbert aside, pulled out the biggest carrots, and threw them in a pile. His mother came to collect them in her basket.

Gilbert muttered and pulled the larger carrots, too. With both of them working, they soon finished the job.

Mrs. Mossman led them to the far end of the garden. "Lester, you and Gilbert finish weeding here. Start with the three long rows of onions."

Gilbert grabbed the weeds, intertwined with the little onions. When he yanked out the weeds, some of the onions came up, too, so he replanted them.

Lester came along and shook his head. "Stupid, can't you do anything right? The ones you stuck back in the ground will never grow. Pull them back out and toss them in the basket at the end of the row."

Gilbert swallowed his irritation and yanked up all his replanted onions, throwing them in the basket.

Lester loomed over him. "Watch me and I'll show you the right way." He pulled the weeds from the outer edges of the rows. "This is the smart way. It leaves half the weeds, but none of the green onions get pulled out."

Gilbert felt like an amateur as Lester stood over him, watching every move. Mrs. Mossman gave them instructions for further work and disappeared into the house. Rather than do any more hoeing or weeding, Lester supervised. He swaggered around the garden like an expert training a new assistant. The hours dragged by, and the sun beat down. Gilbert dripped with sweat while Lester issued his commands from a shady spot under a tree.

Mrs. Mossman called from the back door. "Boys! Wash up and come in for lunch."

Gilbert and Lester raced to the door, eager to be done with garden work. At the wash bucket, Lester elbowed Gilbert to the side. "Get out of the way and wait your turn."

Gilbert hankered to elbow right back, but Mrs. Everal's words echoed in his mind, "You could be a good example."

Mrs. Mossman waited until they had finished their first cheese sandwich before she asked for a report. Lester outlined Gilbert's lack of skill in great detail. "I spent all morning correcting the mistakes he made."

She did not ask Gilbert to give his version, but she smiled and nodded to him. "Well, at least you tried."

Lester grinned. "He was very trying." He made a face at Gilbert when his mother wasn't looking.

Mrs. Mossman handed Gilbert his pay. "Thanks for your work with Lester today. After lunch you can return to the Everals." Gilbert raised an eyebrow and nodded. He would be glad to leave here and work where he was appreciated.

17

A Dip in the Creek

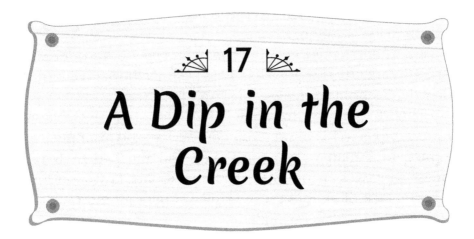

When Gilbert returned to the Everals, Alvin and Frankie ran out to meet him.

"Say yes, please? Pul-ease!" Alvin said.

"Yes, yes, yes!" Frankie said.

"About what? I might say yes if I knew."

Mrs. Everal waved to Gilbert from the kitchen door. "You do know how to swim, don't you?"

"Yes, I learned to swim in our farm pond. And I taught my sister, Annie."

"Today is such a hot day. I told the boys if you agreed to be responsible for the two of them, you all could cool off at the swimming hole."

Frankie pulled on one of Gilbert's arms, and Alvin pulled the other. Both spouted reasons why Gilbert should take them.

Gilbert grinned. "Sounds like fun."

Mrs. Everal handed each of them a towel. "Now you boys stay right with Gilbert. You listen and obey him. Promise?"

"Yes, Mama," said Frankie.

"I promise," said Alvin. And I'll show Gilbert the way to the swimming hole."

"Come home in about two hours. I'm going to run errands in town."

- Choosing Sides -

The three boys set off toward Alum Creek and followed a sun-dappled path along the bank. Squeals and shouts erupted as they neared the wide spot where the water was deep enough for swimming.

"Girls aren't allowed here," Alvin said. "We can keep our clothes dry and go skinny- dipping."

Gilbert glanced at the swimmers to make sure this was true. Boys' heads bobbed in the muddy water, boys splashed other boys, and Lester stood in a line of boys waiting to swing over the water on a grapevine.

Alvin and Frankie stripped while Gilbert hesitated. "Hurry up!" Alvin said.

"We ready," Frankie said.

Gilbert took off his clothes and tossed them on his towel. He noticed a lush vine growing on a nearby tree and warned the boys. "Stay away from the poison ivy right there." They tramped to the bank, worn smooth from many bare feet climbing out of the creek. Alvin wanted to jump from the high bank, but Gilbert led them down the slope to a shallow spot.

The mud squished between their toes, and Frankie squealed. They waded out to the middle till Frankie was up to his neck. Two boys swam behind them and splashed them, laughing. Gilbert swooshed water back at them. Alvin splashed back, too, but Frankie screamed, clutching Gilbert with both arms.

Gilbert tried to calm him. "It's all right, Frankie. I've got you."

"He doesn't know how to swim," Alvin said.

Gilbert bent down to Frankie's eye-level. "Want to learn?"

Frankie peeked around Gilbert and spotted the two boys ready to splash him again. "No!"

"Frankie, don't let a little water scare you. The splashes won't hurt you."

He shook his head. "Frankie all done."

"Want to sit on the bank a while?"

Frankie nodded and all three climbed out. Frankie wrapped his towel around his shoulders and sat on a big rock in the sun.

Gilbert put his face close to Frankie's. "Stay there till I come back to get you, hear?"

Alvin ran to a huge elm tree leaning over the bank. "Can I swing on the vine?" A line of boys waited their turn to swing out over the water on the thick grapevine.

"Wait." Gilbert hurried beside him. "Are you strong enough to hang on the vine all the way to the middle?"

"I've done it before. Papa brought us last summer, and I did it then."

Gilbert bit his lip. "That part looks pretty deep. I'll swing out first to be ready to help you when you splash into the water."

"Whee!" Gilbert swung out and plunged into the water with a big splash. It was deep, so he had to tread water as he waited for Alvin. Gilbert's heart sank when he saw Lester standing in line, looming over little Alvin. Gilbert knew by Lester's smirk he planned something mean. Behind Lester, the two splashers waited their turn.

Alvin grabbed the vine, raced to the edge, and swung out. He slipped off short of the deepest water, so Gilbert swam over to him. Before he reached the boy, Lester swung out and crashed on top of Alvin. Both boys disappeared under the brown water.

Lester came up laughing. "Right on target!"

Gilbert swam to Alvin and pulled him above the surface. "What do you think you're doing? You could drown him or break his arm."

Coughing and crying, Alvin clung to Gilbert. "I wanna go home." A trickle of blood ran from his nose.

Lester's lip curled. "What a baby!"

Gilbert gritted his teeth. "You're a big fat bully. Pick on someone your own size, and you'll be the one to get half-drowned."

Lester guffawed and climbed the bank to swing on the vine again.

Gilbert towed the snuffling boy to where Frankie sat on a rock. "Let's get dressed and go home."

Lester called out, "Cry-baby, cry-baby. Take the baby home."

Alvin, still hiccupping on the way home, asked, "Why did that boy jump on top of me?"

"Because he's a bully. He thinks it's fun to show everyone how big he is."

When Mrs. Everal returned from her errands, Alvin gave a tearful recitation of his ordeal. Frankie tried to get his mother's sympathy, too, but his story of getting splashed couldn't hold a candle to his brother's tale.

Gilbert put an arm around Alvin. "Lester was the boy who landed on top of Alvin, and he did it on purpose. I didn't have a good influence on him."

Alvin rubbed away his tears with the back of his hand. "Why did he do that, Mama? I didn't hurt him or anything."

Mrs. Everal looked thoughtful. "Perhaps his papa never taught him to be kind."

Alvin looked at his mother. "Our papa's very kind, isn't he."

She bent over to hug him. "Yes, he certainly is. And he wants others to be kind, too."

The boys ran off to play, and Mrs. Everal brought out a huge bowl of sour cherries. "Help me pit these so I can bake pies for tomorrow."

Gilbert grinned. "I might take a tax while I work—cherries are something I miss from home."

As they worked, Mrs. Everal revealed more details about the Mossman family. "Lester's father has an anger problem. It's always there, simmering under the surface."

Gilbert said, "Yes, I worked with him. Nothing I did pleased him."

"Maybe I should ask my husband to speak to Jasper about how his son acted. That would lead to a discussion with Jasper about changing his own attitude."

Gilbert popped a cherry into his mouth. "But why is he angry? Seems like he needs a reason."

Mrs. Everal shook her head as she measured flour into a bowl and added dollops of lard to cut in for pie dough. "He grew up in a bad home situation. Before his alcoholic father abandoned them, he beat them."

"I'd be angry if that happened to me." Gilbert hesitated before he asked a follow-up question. "What about Lester's mother?" At Mrs. Everal's quizzical look, Gilbert sketched the details of his morning at the Mossman farm. "Mrs. Mossman didn't see anything wrong with how Lester treated me. It was as if her son could do no wrong. Half of the things he said about me were lies, or at least only half true."

Mrs. Everal's jaw dropped, and she stopped rolling the pie crust. "I had always thought, well, from what Sylvia said, the fault lay in her husband. Lately he has become unreasonably agitated about the Corbin Saloon. This anger rubs off on Lester."

Gilbert bent over his bowl of cherries. "Maybe Lester is a bully because it makes him feel important."

"I'll have a talk with his mother," Mrs. Everal said. "Thanks for telling me this so I will know how we can better pray for Lester. And for Jasper." She followed Gilbert to the door. "By the way, Mr. Everal says he needs you back at the tile factory tomorrow."

18
Surprise Visit

Gilbert left the Everals and grabbed his gunnysack to shop for supper. While buying four loaves of bread at the bakery, he glanced out the front window. He raced out the door when he saw a horse and buggy that looked like Pa's. He rounded the corner, and he could hardly believe his eyes—the man hitching his horse was his father.

"Pa! I'm glad to see you . . . " Gilbert stopped midsentence. His father's stormy look made Gilbert hang back instead of running to hug him. He should have known Pa would be angry, since he had run away.

"Gilbert." Pa's face looked like a dark cloud. "You're coming home with me."

Gilbert's heart sank. He stuck his hands in his pockets and stared at the ground. "But Pa, I have a job. And I found a room on West Street."

"Listen to me, young man." Pa's voice rose a notch. "I've heard from Herman what's going on in Westerville. Have you had anything to do with the Corbin Saloon?"

Gilbert stared with his mouth open. "Ah, yeah." How could Pa know that? "But only a little. I helped him and Mrs. Corbin clean out trash and mop and paint."

"You are never to set foot in that place again." Pa clenched his jaw.

The color drained from Gilbert's face. "At first, I didn't know they were opening a saloon, Pa." He changed the subject. "While you're in town, want to come see where I'm staying?"

"Not really. I don't care, since you're leaving and coming with me."

"It's close, just a few blocks." Gilbert turned and strode toward West Street.

Pa scowled but followed.

As they walked up the steps, Shadow greeted both of them. Gilbert hoped Pa wouldn't care about the mess in the entry. "The three fellows who rent this place let me stay free since I shop and cook for them."

Pa stopped dead in his tracks and raised his eyebrows. "How old are they? They'll lead you astray. You're coming home with me."

Gilbert set his jaw. "Pa, I'm staying here. I want to be on my own. I've got a job, and I'm earning money. I plan to go to Otterbein Academy this fall."

"They know nothing about farming."

Gilbert crossed his arms across his chest. "Maybe I don't want to be a farmer. I've been doing some detective work . . . ."

Pa's anger pulsed between them. Pa turned on his heel and strode toward the buggy. "I can't stay all day. I've got chores to do, cows to milk."

Gilbert followed, wondering what he could say to change Pa's mind. "Did you ask our neighbor, Mr. Smith, to help? He offered. He does his farm chores alone all the time."

Pa whirled to face him. "No, I did not ask him. He's half-drunk most of the time and he'd break the machinery. Or injure himself." Pa stabbed the air. "I have a son to help me. No—I have a son who ought to help me."

Gilbert winced. His father's words hurt.

Pa yanked the horse's bridle from the post. "Any town with a saloon is a bad influence."

"But Westerville is fighting the saloon. I've been to one of the temperance rallies—"

Pa cut him off. "I don't care how many rallies you attend. Get into the buggy."

Gilbert planted his feet and balled his fists. "Pa, I'm not going home!"

Pa raised the horse strap, as if to whip Gilbert. His eyes widened, then narrowed. "Yes, you are."

Gilbert shook his head. No matter what he said, Pa wouldn't listen. There was nothing left to be said.

Pa climbed onto the seat. "Better not wait too long. You may not be welcome." He backed the wagon and snapped the reins. "Giddy up!"

Gilbert jumped back, feeling sorry for his father, yet wounded by his father's words. "Goodbye, Pa." He sighed and watched him drive away.

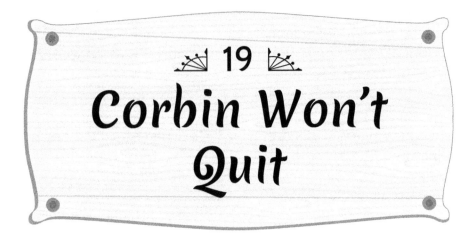

19
Corbin Won't Quit

Gilbert mulled over the conversation with Pa. Could he ever go home? He browned sausage for supper and stirred a batch of biscuits. He wished Annie could see his new cooking skills.

Vern raced in waving a newspaper. "Big news about Corbin's Saloon." Vern perched on a stool and read while Gilbert worked on supper.

> Ohio State Journal, August 5, 1875. Headline: Westerville Whiskey War.
>
> Is Corbin keeping a saloon or a pyrotechnic establishment?
>
> There are more fireworks in his saloon than fire-water. The first powder explosion lifted his roof, shattered his windows, and wrecked his establishment, but after all this he was found behind his counter and the war went on. Then Tuesday night at 9:30 o'clock, a quantity of powder exploded in the west room of Corbin's building with a loud report, raising the roof several inches, and inflicting such general damage that there is not much left to destroy.

Vern shook his head. "How will Corbin stay in business?"

Gilbert banged the wooden spoon on the skillet. "That's terrible."

– Choosing Sides –

When Freddie and Benjie walked in, Vern summarized what he'd finished reading. "It says that another blast completely ruined the Corbin Saloon."

Freddie whooped for joy. "He'll have to leave Westerville now for sure!"

Vern shook his head. "Not so fast, there's more." He continued reading:

> 'Corbin declared he is not finished with saloon-keeping in Westerville.
>
> He has put a down-payment on the Clymer House Hotel on State Street. His plans for it include a saloon and a billiards parlor in the basement."

Vern grinned at Benjie. "Now we won't have to go to Columbus to play billiards."

Gilbert drew his brows together. "What's to keep the vandalizers from driving Corbin out of business in this new location?"

"Good question." Freddie collected plates and silverware to set the table. "But I think I know the answer. The Clymer House is between two other buildings, so the vandalizers wouldn't blow up the whole area just to hurt Corbin."

"Listen to this." Vern continued reading:

> "'Maybe Westerville could afford to suspend hostilities against a one-horse beer saloon long enough to dig out the perpetrators. We commend the City Council for offering a six-hundred-dollar reward.'"

Gilbert carried the pot of sausage gravy to the table. "Six hundred dollars! That's big money."

Freddie snickered. "Are you going to try to collect that reward?"

"Why not? Who wants to help me?"

Freddie filled his plate and grinned at Gilbert. "You may be a good cook, but you're not sneaky enough to catch whoever it is that's been vandalizing Corbin's place."

Vern shook his head. "Gil almost caught two prowlers the other night when they egged the place, but he was outnumbered. Count me in. I could use that reward money."

Benjie took a second helping and chimed in. "Corbin deserves to have them pay for his damages, so I'd like to help catch them, too."

Gilbert lowered his voice. "I have a strong suspicion of who's doing this, but we have to catch them in the act."

Vern's eyes lit up. "Let's do another stakeout at Corbin's."

"Right. The more often we're there, the more likely we'll catch somebody."

Freddie tore open three more biscuits and covered them with sausage gravy. "You three are wasting your time. The constable will stake out the new place."

Vern shook his head. "They weren't at his old place when we went last week."

Freddie paused, a big bite of biscuit and gravy halfway to his mouth. "I know a better way to spend your time. How about if all three of you come out to the mass temperance meeting tonight?"

Benjie shook his head. "No thanks. Preachers put me to sleep."

Vern stood and stretched. "Maybe next time."

Gilbert was easy to convince, since he expected Rose would be there. "I'll go. It'll please my father. Today he's very much displeased with me."

"How do you know that?" Freddie asked.

"He came to town to take me back home, but I wouldn't go with him."

Vern stacked the dishes. "His little boy is growing up. You go to the meeting, and I'll wash the dishes and pots. It's my turn anyway."

20
Bar to Heaven

Freddie and Gilbert stood in the back of the chapel watching families file in for the meeting. Gilbert waved to Mr. and Mrs. Goodspeed and their girls and pulled Freddie toward them. "That's the Goodspeed family. He owns the farm tool store. Let's sit next to them, and I'll introduce you afterwards."

Gilbert knew it would be hard to focus on the preaching with Rose sitting right next to him, especially since the pew was so crowded that her arm touched his. Gilbert's heart rate rose as she sang the hymns in her lilting soprano. All too soon, a tall man with a dark beard stood to preach.

Rose whispered, "That's Reverend Robertson. We like him the best of all the temperance preachers." Gilbert recognized him as one of the leaders in the crowd on Corbin's opening day. That was one strike against him.

"My text tonight is taken from the book of Genesis, chapter four." Reverend Robertson's deep voice reminded Gilbert of his grandfather. "Two brothers brought gifts to God. Abel brought what God had commanded, a lamb from his flock. Cain decided his own idea was better, so he brought the best of his garden harvest. God accepted the sacrifice of the lamb as payment for Abel's sin, but God rejected Cain's offering. This made Cain angry. The Lord said to Cain, 'Why are you angry, and why has your face fallen? If you do well, will you not be accepted?' The Lord told Cain to do right, and he would be accepted. I ask you, did Cain change so God would accept his offering? No. Cain would not change. He thought his own way was just fine."

Gilbert hung his head, identifying himself with Cain. They had both gone ahead with their own ideas, and it drove them from their homes.

Reverend Robertson pounded the pulpit, making Gilbert jump. "Cain did not change his offering, though God gave him the chance. In an angry rage he killed his brother Abel. What an evil deed! When God asked Cain, 'Where is Abel your brother?' Cain's retort was a lie, 'I do not know.' Then Cain asked God an insolent question, one that still echoes in our ears. 'Am I my brother's keeper?' Cain thought the answer would be no."

Reverend Robertson leaned forward. "We should ask ourselves that same question. Do we care enough about our fellow man to hold him back from an early grave? Do we care enough to stand against the ones who want to bring the temptations of ardent spirits into our town? We have abolished the slave trade from our land—do we care enough to abolish this evil which enslaves men? Are we our brother's keeper?"

Gilbert's heart pounded as he tried to answer that question. Reverend Robertson presented the temperance issue as caring for others. The temperance people cared. The Corbins didn't care. If they cared about the citizens of Westerville, they would close their saloon.

Reverend Robertson waved a paper for the crowd to see. "This poem was written by a lifetime prisoner, and it is titled, The Saloon. Let me read it to you.

> 'The saloon is sometimes called a bar;
> That's true.
> A bar to heaven, a door to hell,
> Whoever named it, named it well.
> A bar to manliness and wealth,

A door to want and broken health,
A bar to honor, pride, and fame;
A door to grief and sin and shame,
A bar to hope, a bar to prayer;
A door to darkness and despair,
A bar to honored, useful life;
A door to brawling, senseless strife.
A bar to all that's true and brave;
A door to every drunkard's grave.
A bar to joys that home imparts,
A door to tears and aching hearts.
A bar to heaven, a door to hell,
Whoever named it, named it well.'"

The crowd murmured their approval. Gilbert closed his eyes. The preaching had turned his thoughts around, and he was seeing things in a new way.

Rose touched Gilbert's arm and whispered, "See, I told you he was good."

After Reverend Robertson closed the meeting in prayer, Gilbert introduced his friend. "Freddie, meet the family who invited a hungry farm boy to a fine meal when he wandered into town."

Mr. Goodspeed laughed. "Gilbert almost slipped out the back door of the church, but I blocked his way. Nice to meet you, . . . um, what did you say your name was?"

"Frederick. But call me Freddie. We've adopted this farm boy, too."

"These are my daughters, Iva and Rose." The girls smiled and nodded.

Rose asked, "What did you both think of the preaching?"

Freddie smiled and gave a thumbs up signal.

Gilbert said, "I think if I come to any more of these mass meetings, I'll soon be marching in Westerville's temperance parade." This made Rose smile and Freddie laugh.

Mrs. Goodspeed called to them as they turned to go. “Hope to see you at the meeting tomorrow night.”

Gilbert rubbed his chin. Any more preaching like he’d heard tonight would change his mind about the Corbins and their saloon. He didn’t want his opinion to change so drastically.

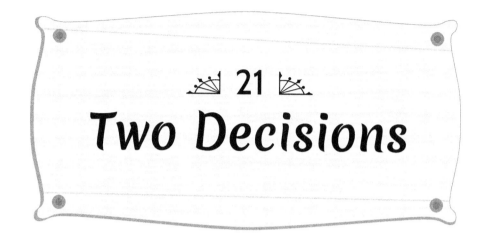

21
Two Decisions

Gilbert wished he could talk to Rose—alone—just the two of them. Twice he had accidentally met her while they shopped for groceries, but they didn't get to have much real conversation. He'd been to two temperance meetings, and they'd said a few words. However, with everyone around, they couldn't talk in private. He decided to ask Freddie for help, since he had a girlfriend.

After supper, Gilbert cornered Freddie in the kitchen. "I need your advice, friend to friend."

Freddie kept washing the dishes. "I'm all ears. Dry the dishes while you tell me all about it."

Gilbert wiped plates and put them away. "I'd like to ask Rose Goodspeed for a date. Where's a good place in town to take her?"

"It has to be a classy place, since her father is on the city council."

Gilbert bit his lip. "Maybe he'll say no."

"He might veto a date with the two of you alone. How about a double date?"

Gilbert brightened. "That's a good idea—could you and your girl come too? Where shall we go?"

"How much do you want to spend?"

Gilbert rubbed the back of his neck. "Not very much—I'm saving for school."

Freddie set the pot on the drainboard for Gilbert to dry. "Maybe a restaurant in Columbus—"

Gilbert broke in. "It has to be here in town. I know her father wouldn't let her ride the train to Columbus."

"The answer might be in the newspaper I read before supper." Freddie headed to the living room. He pointed to a notice on the back page: 'The Ladies of the Westerville Methodist Church will hold an Ice Cream Sociable next Thursday evening."

Gilbert looked up with a big smile. "That's perfect, since the church is two blocks from her house."

Freddie stretched out in the chair. "The fee for attending is usually thirty cents per person. Can you afford that?"

"Yes, barely." Gilbert hummed a tune. "I'm going to invite her tonight." He smoothed his pants and combed his hair. "Like my Pa used to say, make hay while the sun shines."

Freddie looked up from his paper and grinned. "Gil, sometimes you surprise me."

Gilbert had second thoughts on the short walk to the Goodspeeds. He decided he should ask Mr. Goodspeed first and then ask Rose.

Iva answered his knock. "Well, if it isn't Gilbert. What brings you here tonight?"

Gilbert swallowed. "I've come to speak to your father. Is he available?"

"No, he's at a city council meeting tonight. But you can come in and talk to the rest of us."

Gilbert hesitated and shook his head. "I'll come back tomorrow evening, if that would be better."

Iva half smiled, as if she thought him crazy. "He'll be here tomorrow evening."

Gilbert thanked her and hurried down the steps. He was relieved he had another day to figure out what to say to Mr.

Goodspeed. On his way home, he detoured to investigate the new Corbin House Hotel on State Street. Uptown was nearly deserted, but Gilbert glimpsed a slender figure disappearing down an alley. He remembered the fellows at work saying something about a stranger hanging around. Did the man have a connection to the vandalisms?

When Gilbert arrived at Corbin's place, the lights were on and the door was open, so Gilbert poked his head inside.

Mr. Corbin spotted him and said, "Gilbert, you're just the boy I wanted to see. Come in, and I'll show you around Corbin House." He led the way to the dining area. "We'll run a restaurant here along with the hotel. We've got fifteen rooms upstairs. It's a prime location and we'll be able to recoup our investment in five years."

Gilbert looked around and nodded. "It looks pretty good."

Mr. Corbin led him to the basement next. "I hope to have a saloon and billiards parlor down here."

"I read about that in the paper." Gilbert wrinkled his nose at the damp, dingy room.

"The temperance crowd paid me a visit and said they'd make my hotel a success if I'd desist from opening a saloon." Mr. Corbin's guffaw echoed in the empty room. "I won't change my plans. My success doesn't depend on Westerville, but on my own hard work."

Gilbert cringed at Mr. Corbin's attitude.

Mr. Corbin pointed to a trash-filled corner. "This basement needs work—it's dirty and dark. I'll pay you to help me clean and paint down here."

Gilbert hesitated. He needed the money—the Academy cost twelve dollars a semester and he couldn't work for Mr. Everal after school started. But if he said yes, he'd be helping the Corbins open a saloon. He could not do that. "I'm pretty busy with the jobs I have already, Mr. Corbin."

Mr. Corbin arched his bushy eyebrows. "Hmph. You're passing up good money."

Gilbert bade him goodbye and strode home. He might come up short of money, but if he did, God would provide it. He remembered a story from Sunday School about Peter finding a coin in a fish's mouth. His decision would please Rose and Mr. Goodspeed. And his father. Most important of all, it would please God.

22 Permission Granted

Gilbert worked at the tile factory all morning, as usual, and shopped for supper right after lunch. August heat hovered over the whole town, making Gilbert wish for a breeze. He sighed as he remembered the cooling breeze on the farm.

Gilbert had a hard time getting the stove started, since he was low on kindling. He wished he knew how to fix something besides a roast since the long simmering time added more heat to the stuffy house. He sat on the porch to open the surprise letter he'd received from Annie.

Dear Gilbert,

Aunt Ruby and I have had a really good summer. I wish you could have been here to see my first cherry pie—it was almost too beautiful to eat! It had a lattice top, just like Ma used to make. Being with Aunt Ruby is almost like being with Ma, since she gives me hugs and advice all the time.

Pa wrote us that you'd gone to Westerville—what a big surprise. He said I could write to you by putting West Street on the envelope. That means you're already well-known in town, I *suppose. Pa didn't say, but I could see that he's upset with you. But he was that way before you left. I really miss you—I have nobody to boss around!*

Love, your sister,
Annie

Gilbert put the letter back in the envelope and stared out the window. He tried to swallow past the lump in his throat. Would he ever go back home? Maybe Pa would keep Annie home from school, now that Gilbert wasn't there to do all of the work.

He sat up straighter. He would not lose sight of his goal of going to Otterbein Academy in the fall. Annie would do a fine job of cooking the meals and doing all the other chores Ma used to do. Annie had always been a homebody, so she wouldn't care about staying home from school. He was glad Annie missed him. He missed her, too.

Suppertime discussion centered on Corbin's new building. "Corbin's still determined to have a saloon and billiards parlor," Gilbert said. "He showed me the basement—what a dank and cold cave! It needs a lot of work. He asked me to help, but I've had my eyes opened."

Freddie clapped. "Good for you, Gil. Aren't you glad you went to the Temperance meeting?"

Gilbert raised his palm as if to stop a wrong idea. "I'm not ready yet to join the hecklers and temperance marchers."

Vern rubbed his hands together. "And remember, we're still trying to catch the vandals who've wrecked the other Corbin building."

Gilbert nodded. "But not tonight. I'm headed to ask Rose's father if I can take her to the Ice Cream Sociable on Thursday. He wasn't there last night."

Vern shook his head. "How did you get a girlfriend already?"

Freddie chuckled. "Gilbert is full of surprises."

– Choosing Sides –

Gilbert whistled as he strode toward the Goodspeeds. The air had cooled, and the trees rustled with a brisk breeze.

Iva answered the door and invited Gilbert to the parlor where the rest of the family was gathered.

After they exchanged greetings, Gilbert glanced at Rose. Would it be better if he spoke to her father privately? Too late now. He bit his lip and cleared his throat. "Mr. Goodspeed, I'd like permission to take your daughter Rose to the upcoming Ice Cream Sociable."

Before Mr. Goodspeed had a chance to answer, Iva drew in a long breath. "Oooh. Can I go, too, Papa?"

Rose glanced at her father and shook her head.

"Iva, the invitation was for Rose." Mr. Goodspeed turned to Gilbert. "It's fine with me if Rose would like to be your guest at this festive event."

Rose's cheeks blushed pink. "Yes, I would really like that."

Mrs. Goodspeed looked up from her needlework. "I've heard that the ladies of the Methodist Church make very tasty ice cream."

Mr. Goodspeed grinned. "What day did you say it was? Perhaps Mrs. Goodspeed and I will join you."

Rose slumped and sighed.

"And me, too, Papa," Iva said.

Gilbert had hoped for a chance to be alone with Rose, or at least away from those who would listen to their conversation. "It's next Thursday evening at seven."

Mr. Goodspeed said, "Fine. We'll see you then."

Rose stood and led Gilbert to the door. Iva jumped up, too, but her father called her back to sit beside him. When Iva flounced into the chair, Rose smirked at her.

Rose stepped on the porch with Gilbert and put a hand on his arm. "Thank you for inviting me to the Sociable."

Gilbert put his hand over hers. "I can't think of anyone else I'd rather go with."

He wanted to say more, but Iva stuck her head out the door. "Goodnight, Gilbert."

Rose snatched her hand back and glared at Iva, then said, "Goodnight, Gilbert."

Gilbert smiled all the way home.

23
Super Sleuths

Late one night, Gilbert, Vern, and Benjie dressed in dark clothes and headed toward the new Corbin House. They used the back alleys and stayed in the shadows. A soft breeze brought night sounds—crickets and tree frogs. As the three figures sneaked toward State Street, six neighborhood dogs alerted their owners, but no one came out to check.

Vern whispered, "I've got rags for blindfolds and gags."

Benjie tapped a heavy walking stick down with each step.

"What's the stick for?" Gilbert asked.

Benjie jabbed the stick into the ground. "To trip them when they run past our hiding place."

Gilbert lifted his rope. "You trip the villains, and I'll tie them up." He had high hopes of catching the vandals and earning reward money.

"I think we should split up," Vern said. "We'll have a better chance."

"We should stay close enough to hear each other yell for help, though." Gilbert knew how strong the two suspects were. He'd outlined for Benjie and Vern the many reasons he guessed Jasper and son Lester Mossman were the culprits.

No dogs barked when they reached Corbin's new place on State Street. Gilbert said, "Evidently Mr. Corbin didn't take my suggestion to get a guard dog."

Before they split up, Gilbert gave directions. "A whistle means come help, and an owl call means run from the scene." They agreed that they'd spend at least three hours on the stakeout, though nobody had a watch.

Vern hunched in the bushes two houses down from Corbin House. Benjie hid in the alley between two buildings across the street, and Gilbert crept to the back yard of the Corbin House through a narrow walkway beside the house.

Gilbert investigated the grassy area behind the Corbin's new building. A night sky full of stars shone enough light to see a young maple tree with low branches, easy to climb. Gilbert checked—no one was hiding there. A row of butterfly bushes reminded him of one in his own front yard. It had been his mother's favorite, but the flowers always made Gilbert sneeze. He backed away, since sneezing was not good for stakeouts.

He squatted behind the building and imagined various scenarios. He'd tie up Jasper and Lester with his rope, and he would be the hero and share the reward money.

He heard a whistle, so he grabbed the rope and ran to the street to help Benjie and Vern. But instead of his friends, a tall, slender man paced the sidewalk toward him. He jumped back into the shadows, hoping he'd not been seen. He raced back and squeezed behind the butterfly bushes. The slender man rounded the back corner of the building and stopped.

Gilbert held his breath.

"Come out, wherever you are!" The man stepped five steps closer to Gilbert's hiding place.

Gilbert's heart pounded. Should he stay in the dark and hope the man was bluffing?

The man stepped closer. "Give yourself up or else."

"Aaaa-CHOO!" Gilbert froze. The sneeze had given away his hiding place.

The man raced toward him. "I know you're there. Don't move!"

Gilbert jumped up. He ran two steps and fell flat on his face.

"Stop. You can't get away."

Gilbert untangled his foot from the rope. He crawled away, but a strong hand clamped his arm and yanked him to his feet. "What are you planning to do with that rope, you hooligan?"

Gilbert's heart raced so fast he couldn't catch his breath. "I . . . I'm trying to . . . catch the vandals. The ones who've been . . . wrecking Mr. Corbin's building."

The man's grip tightened. "A ridiculous story. I don't believe it. I'm marching you to jail." He shoved Gilbert toward the street.

"Whoo, whoo!" Gilbert signaled his friends.

The man stopped and pulled Gilbert toward him. "Is that a signal?"

"W-who are y-you, sir?" Gilbert hoped he'd covered the signal with his question.

"I'm asking the questions around here. Who are you?"

"I'm Gilbert Freeman. And I'm telling the truth. Ask Mr. Corbin about me. I even worked for him."

"That doesn't mean you're not the one vandalizing. Maybe you have a grudge. You're spending the night in jail." The man marched Gilbert five blocks to the new City Council building. Gilbert's legs felt heavier with every step.

He dragged his feet as the man pushed him into the brick building. The official on duty stared at him. "Name?"

Gilbert wished he could give a made-up name but tossed the idea aside. "Gilbert Freeman."

The official wrote Gilbert's name in a large record book. "His offense?"

The man tapped the record book. "Trespassing on private property."

"Is this the first suspect you've apprehended for the Corbin case?"

"Yep. Though the kid says he's innocent."

"I've heard that line before. Bring him back to the holding cell, and I'll lock him up."

After the door slammed behind him, Gilbert felt his way to the narrow bed and stretched out. He felt sick to his stomach, and his head ached. How had things gone so wrong?

24
An Invitation

"Good morning." The jailer, an older man who walked with a shuffle, opened the cell and slid a tray to Gilbert. "Here's your breakfast." The strong, musty smell of the jail made Gilbert's stomach turn over at the thought of eating oatmeal.

"Thank you, sir." Gilbert had slept little and had no idea how he would get out of jail. "What happens next?"

"The Mayor hears your case at nine. If you have any witnesses, they may speak on your behalf." The door clanged shut, and the jailer shuffled out of sight.

Gilbert's heart sank. Nobody knew he was in jail, except Vern and Benjie. They could tell Mr. Everal, but Gilbert didn't want his employer to know he was in jail. He could lose his job.

He forced the cold oatmeal down his throat and returned the bowl to the tray. He sank down, with his head in his hands, to wait till nine o'clock. Pa would be ashamed to see him in jail. Rose would never go anywhere with him if she knew he'd been in jail.

The door clanked open. "Hello, Gilbert. What in the world are you doing here?"

"Mr. Corbin." Gilbert jumped up. "My buddies and I were trying to capture— "

"You were trying to capture the crooks, but you got captured instead. Ha! "

"I hoped to earn reward money."

"With a rope?"

Gilbert flushed. It did sound ridiculous. "I'm innocent."

"The detective told me to come down and press charges. I never expected to see you."

"I wouldn't vandalize your place." Gilbert shook his head. "I've got a job, and I'm late, so I hope the mayor takes my case first."

"They don't have any other cases. I'm angry Westerville hasn't caught anyone yet. I'm not pressing charges, so you can leave as soon as I sign the papers."

Gilbert lowered his voice. "I think I know who's been doing all the vandalism."

"You do?" Corbin leaned forward, a gleam in his eyes. "Was it one of Westerville's upstanding citizens? I'd give a barrel of beer to see Hanby or Robertson in jail."

Gilbert shook his head. "No. A troublemaker I work with."

Corbin shrugged and pulled at his beard, which was already thin. "You should go after the reward money. Do the legwork. Catch the man."

Gilbert's eyes brightened, and he thought of how he could catch Jasper. "I'll try."

Corbin signed the papers, and Gilbert raced to work, covering the eight blocks in seven minutes. He reported to Mr. Everal, panting. "Sorry . . . I'm late . . . to work. I . . . was detained . . . against my will."

To Gilbert's relief, Mr. Everal's quizzical look was not followed by any questions. He said, "Jasper had to haul the tile cart for three hours. He's angry, so be prepared."

Jasper's lip curled when he saw Gilbert. "So glad the lazy boy finally came to work. I've done your job all morning, so you can pay me half your pay."

Gilbert shook his head and stacked tiles onto the cart, usually Jasper's job.

"You come late and try to take my job?" He elbowed Gilbert out of the way, knocking two tiles from his hands. "See, you're too clumsy to do it right. Why Everal hired you I'll never know. My son Lester could do better than you."

Gilbert stepped back. "I was trying to help."

Jasper finished stacking the tiles on the cart. "Roll it away, cart-boy."

With great effort, Gilbert kept his mouth closed and rolled the cart to the drying shed. As he unloaded it, he imagined making Jasper spend time in jail in the near future. He planned how he would spend the reward money. He wouldn't have to work when he attended Otterbein Academy. He would learn how to be a detective.

At midday, Mr. Everal paid him half as much as usual and sent him on his way with no questions. Gilbert dragged his weary legs to West Street, brought in the mail, and sat down to rest. He was startled to find a letter with his name on it—a letter from his father. He ripped open the envelope, hoping his father wasn't still angry. His mouth dropped open as he read the few lines. "This Friday, I am hosting an important family event. Please come join your sister, aunts, uncles, cousins, grandparents, and other relatives at the farm. Hope to see you then. Pa."

Shadow hopped on his lap, and Gilbert stroked him—a purring cat eased his tensions. What was the big event? Maybe the family was gathering so everyone could pressure him to come back home to stay. Should he go or not? Pa had threatened that he might not be welcome. He closed his eyes to think and woke up much later, with Shadow still on his lap. The nap refreshed him, but he was no closer to deciding the knotty question.

While he worked on supper, Gilbert reread the letter. Should he go? Would he and Pa argue again?

Vern burst into the room. "Hey, Gilbert. You spent the night in jail?" He cackled at the idea.

Gilbert made a face. "Yes, no thanks to you."

"You signaled me and Benjie to leave, so we didn't try to rescue you."

"I know. That would've made it worse. The man that nabbed me thought I was trying to vandalize Corbin's new place."

"With a rope?" Vern laughed. "So how did they treat you?"

"Locked me in a cell with a hard bed and no pillow. Gave me cold oatmeal for breakfast. But Mr. Corbin came and told them I was not the culprit." Gilbert snickered. "But I may get part of the reward money after all, if my suspicion is correct about the vandals."

Vern rubbed his hands together. "Want Benjie and me to help you?"

Gilbert rolled his eyes. "Yeah, like the last time you helped?"

Over supper, Gilbert shared the letter from his father. Freddie thought he should go home for the event. Vern and Benjie thought he should not. Nobody wanted him to move back to the farm. They joked about how they would starve without his cooking.

Gilbert couldn't decide. Today was Wednesday, so he had one more day to decide about Pa's invitation. He was terrible at making decisions.

25
The Ice Cream Sociable

Gilbert sat up in bed the next morning and reminded himself—this evening he was taking Rose to the Ice Cream Sociable. Was Rose thinking about it, too?

At the tile factory, he bumbled through his tasks, giving Jasper more reasons to mock and yell at him.

At supper, Benjie tasted the gravy and asked, "Gil, did you forget the salt?"

Vern held up a burned green bean. "He forgot to put water in the bean pot."

Freddie studied Gilbert and grinned. "He has his mind on other things—or on a certain girl."

Gilbert's cheeks turned pink. He swallowed a bite of mashed potatoes. "And the potatoes are lumpy, too. Sorry. It's not my best effort."

Benjie said, "We forgive you. It's the night you're taking your girl to that shindig at the Methodist Church, right?"

Gilbert grinned and stood. "Right. And I need to get ready."

Freddie waved a hand at the table. "We'll clean up. Leave everything to us."

Vern asked, "Would you like to wear my blue shirt and vest?"

"Would I? Yes! Rose won't even recognize me."

Thirty minutes later, Gilbert, washed, combed, and neatly dressed, hiked the four blocks to the Goodspeeds and knocked on the door. His heart raced as he waited.

Rose, looking as fresh as a rosebud in a pale pink dress, opened the door. "Gilbert. Come in and say hello to everyone."

Iva peeked out from the parlor. "Oooh! You have a new shirt. I was getting tired of that old green one."

Rose turned to glare. "Iva, keep your opinion to yourself ." She glided toward the parlor. "Gilbert, Mama and Papa want to have a word with you."

A shiver went down Gilbert's back.

Mr. Goodspeed stood and shook hands with Gilbert. "It's a lovely evening for the Sociable."

Mrs. Goodspeed looked up from the needlework in her lap. "We were tempted to come along."

Iva flounced into the room from the doorway. "But I volunteered to be your chaperone."

Rose bit her lip. "We hardly need one. We'll be in public the whole time."

Mrs. Goodspeed put another stitch in her pillow cover. "Never mind that, dear. It's good that Iva is going. We don't want tongues to wag, do we?"

Rose sighed. "No, Mama. Can we . . . may we go now?"

Mrs. Goodspeed nodded. "Wear your capes, girls. The night air will get chilly, and you're having ice cream."

"But, Mama, it's a warm evening." Iva rolled her eyes. She looked at her father, who nodded. She sighed. "All right. I'll get the capes."

Iva tagged behind Gilbert and Rose, who walked side by side along the street. Gilbert asked Rose, "Have you ever been to an ice cream sociable?"

Rose fingered the string of blue beads around her neck. "This is my first. The Methodist Church began them only last year."

– Choosing Sides –

Gilbert said, "I've heard they'll have three flavors of ice cream. It will be hard to choose."

"I hope they have chocolate," Iva called.

Gilbert's face lit up. "I have an idea. We can share each of our bowls of ice cream."

Rose grinned. "What a good idea. That way we could try two flavors."

Iva's voice rose with a demand. "You'd better give me a big bite, too,"

"We might." Rose's eyes narrowed. "If you don't pester us too much."

Gilbert guided them to the ticket booth at the front of the church. "Two, please."

Rose glanced at Iva. "You did bring your own money?"

Gilbert hadn't thought about bringing enough for Iva. Maybe he should offer to give her his ticket.

"Don't worry." Iva lifted her chin and pulled three dimes from her tiny pocketbook. "You don't have to buy my ticket. Papa gave me money."

Couples and families sauntered around the grounds of the church. Colorful tables had empty bowls stacked ten high beside containers of spoons. Gilbert, Rose, and Iva headed toward the back, where a crowd watched three young men turning cranks on ice cream freezers.

Rose read the sign in front of the first freezer. "Blackberry." She turned to Gilbert. "Let's choose that one first."

Iva walked to the next one. "Here's what I choose—chocolate. I'm waiting here till it's ready."

Gilbert guided Rose to the edge of the crowd. "We can talk here without Iva listening. I want your opinion."

Rose moved a little closer and lowered her voice. "What is it?"

Gilbert bit his lip. "I got a letter from my pa. I'll read it, and you tell me what you think. 'This Friday, I am hosting an important family event. Please come join your sister, aunts, uncles, cousins, grandparents, and other relatives at the farm. Hope to see you then. Pa.'"

Rose looked up with a smile. "I think that something wonderful is going to happen and that your pa wants you to be there."

Gilbert yearned to tell her more about himself, so he blurted out facts he'd never told her before. "I ran away from home after Pa and me had a big argument. I haven't been back home since then."

Rose's eyes widened. "It must sadden you to be split apart from your family." Her voice trembled.

Gilbert knew Rose would listen to his story with sympathy. "After Ma died, Pa made me quit school and do all the things she used to do. But that's not the main reason I ran away. He acted like he hated me."

Rose reached out to touch his hand but glanced at the crowd and pulled back. "I'm sorry, Gilbert."

"The last thing Pa said to me was that I may not be welcome if I come back. I wonder if he'll be glad to see me."

"Of course, he will. He invited you back."

Gilbert shook his head. "Pa and I always end up arguing."

"Iva and I often have different ideas from our parents. That's why we like talking to you." Rose swallowed hard. "You asked for my opinion—I think you should go."

Iva ran up to them, a smear of chocolate ice cream on her chin. "The chocolate is the best. I almost saved you a bite—"

Gilbert cut in with a tease. "You are saving a dribble for later—right on your chin." He took Rose's hand and stepped toward the blackberry ice cream table. "Let's get our ice cream now."

Iva wiped her chin and stuck out her tongue at Gilbert's and Rose's backs. She took two steps to follow them when a girlfriend grabbed her hand. "Come see who's here."

"Ohh. Tell me," Iva said. She and her friend ran through the crowd holding hands.

– Choosing Sides –

Gilbert and Rose carried their bowl of blackberry ice cream to one of the tables and sat down across from each other.

"You get the first bite," Gilbert said, sliding the bowl toward her.

Rose took a dainty taste. "Mmm. I'm glad we chose blackberry." She slid the bowl back.

Gilbert took a large spoonful, then held his head. "Oww."

Rose giggled. "Serves you right. If we're to share equally, then I should get three bites to every one of yours."

Gilbert chuckled. "You sound like one of those wild-eyed women who are marching for the right to vote." He slid the bowl across to Rose. "Take as many spoonsful as you like."

Rose ignored the ice cream and sputtered a reply. "Why shouldn't women be allowed to vote? Tell me one good reason."

Gilbert, hoping to settle the discussion, said in a calm voice, "Women should not be allowed to vote because they are too easily swayed. Male politicians would take advantage of them."

Rose crossed her arms and narrowed her gaze. "Yes, women are weak, which is why their drunken husbands beat them up and threaten to kill them. But if they could vote, they'd gain political power. Then laws could be passed to help them."

Gilbert snorted and shook his head. "You've been listening to crusaders like Mother Stewart for too long."

Rose's jaw dropped. "Are you saying you don't agree with the temperance movement?"

Gilbert looked around, hoping to see a way to change the subject, but he found nothing. He plunged ahead. "Drinking too much alcohol can ruin a family, so I agree up to a point. But giving women the vote is going too far."

Rose shoved the bowl of ice cream back toward Gilbert. "I'm a woman, or at least I will be when I'm old enough to vote—if women ever get to vote. Maybe I've let you sway me too much."

Gilbert swallowed hard. “I’m sorry you got mad at me. Let’s eat our ice cream before it melts.” He slid the bowl back toward Rose. “It’s your turn.”

Rose slid the bowl back and stood. “You can have the rest. I’ve lost my appetite. I’m going to find Iva.”

Gilbert hurried after her. “Rose. Wait.” He wished he had kept his mouth shut about women’s suffrage.

They found Iva laughing with three friends. Rose grabbed her sister’s arm. “It’s time to leave.”

Iva pulled away. “Don’t be silly. Gilbert, can we stay longer?”

Gilbert had no safe answer, so he said nothing.

“Gilbert doesn’t get to decide,” Rose snapped. “My vote is what counts, and we’re going home. Now.”

Iva looked at Rose and then at Gilbert. “Beware the wrath of Rose. Beware the wrath of Rose.” This chant made Rose’s face turn bright red.

Iva said a quick goodbye to her friends as Rose dragged her toward home. The girls walked side by side, and Gilbert trailed behind. He wondered if Rose would accept an apology.

Iva ran inside when they reached the Goodspeed home.

Before Rose stepped over the threshold, Gilbert called to her. “I’m sorry for whatever I said that upset you.”

“You told me how you feel about women in general. That’s enough for me. Goodnight.” She turned and ran inside.

Gilbert slouched back to West Street. He went straight to his bedroom. The last thing he wanted to do was to let Freddie and Vern and Benjie know how he’d botched his first date.

26 Explosion

Gilbert bolted upright in bed and stared out the window into the dark—a loud explosion had wakened him from a sound sleep. He puzzled over what could have caused so much noise in the middle of the night.

Freddie hollered up the stairs, "Did you hear that gigantic BOOM? I'm going uptown—something big happened. Anybody coming with me?"

As soon as he'd pulled on pants, shoes, and shirt, Gilbert raced with his friends toward State Street. Others joined them, some with lanterns, though the oil street lamps still glowed. Gilbert stared as they neared the Corbin's new building—the front door hung on one hinge, the windows were broken, and part of the roof lay in the street.

Gilbert asked a pajama-clad man, "Was anyone killed?"

He shrugged. "I don't know. Nobody's come out yet."

Gilbert called to Vern. "The whole Corbin family lives in there. Bet they need help. Let's go."

Inside, the slanted floor was littered with chunks of plaster. Mrs. Corbin spotted them and ran to pull on Gilbert's arm. "Help me! Osca and Clem . . . look. That was their bedroom—it crashed into the basement."

Gilbert and Vern stepped over plaster and lathe strips. Vern stared into the gaping hole in the floor. "I can't see anything."

Gilbert clutched his chest. "Listen—hear that? It's a child crying."

Mrs. Corbin, at his elbow, was in hysterics. "Osca, are you all right? Is Clem there with you?"

A child's voice said, "Mama! We can't find the stairs. The basement is full of boards and plaster."

Gilbert shouted into the darkness. "Stay where you are, we'll dig you out." Gilbert and Vern hurried to the basement stairs. They kicked plaster off each step and descended into the darkness.

As they reached the basement level, Gilbert grabbed Vern's arm. "Hurry. I smell smoke—there's a fire down here."

Vern peered into the darkness. "This basement's a disaster. Osca? Where are you?" They heard a faint cry, followed by a boy's voice calling for help.

Gilbert pulled away chunks of plaster to make a path. "We're coming."

Vern pointed. "That's where they are—under the hole in the ceiling." He pulled broken lath strips from the pile of debris.

Gilbert heard cries as he pulled a heavy board back. He glimpsed the edge of a blanket, then two feet. "Osca?" He pulled away more plaster chunks.

Osca sobbed. "I thought we'd never get out!" She pointed to a pile of boards. "My brother's over there."

Gilbert helped her climb out. Other than scratches on her face, she seemed unhurt.

Vern pulled the boards and plaster from around the Corbin boy and soon had him free. He had a deep cut on his face and acted dazed. Vern grasped his hand. "Come with me. We'll get you to safety."

After they climbed back to the main floor with the two children, three Franklin Fire Guards strode toward them carrying buckets of water. The first one in line, a burly man with a beard, asked, "Any fires down there?"

"Maybe. There's plenty of smoke," Gilbert said.

The three men headed down the stairs as Mrs. Corbin shouted from a back room. "Help!"

Vern led the two children outside while Gilbert hurried to help her.

She hung on Gilbert's arm, sobbing. "Help! It's Harry—he's out cold. We have to get him out of here."

Mr. Corbin lay across a doorway. His forehead had a deep cut and the bruises on his lip looked as if several teeth had been knocked out. He moaned as Gilbert and Mrs. Corbin knelt beside him. He blinked and turned an unfocused gaze at Gilbert. "Wha . . . What happened?"

Mrs. Corbin sobbed and threw herself across his chest. "You're alive."

Gilbert put a hand under the injured man's shoulder. "There's been an explosion. Try to sit up."

"Why?" Mr. Corbin gaped as one who had awakened from a bad dream.

Mrs. Corbin leaned close to his face. "Harry! We have to get out of here!"

Gilbert and Mrs. Corbin supported the dazed man, half-dragging him outside.

Crowds milled around, craning their necks, guessing the cause of the loud noise. The five Corbin children huddled with an older woman. Gilbert guessed she was the grandma who took care of them while the parents worked.

Trembling, Mrs. Corbin turned to stare at the building. "Corbin House is a wreck! The roof is in the street." She covered her face with her hands and sobbed.

A portly Franklin Fire Guard tried to comfort her with quiet words.

She continued to sob. "We all could have been killed with that blast." Her voice rose to a screech. "I'll get even with those temperance fanatics. They say they're protecting the precious youth of Westerville from the evils of alcohol, but they're endangering everyone in this town."

Mrs. Corbin clung to her husband, tears streaming down her face. He was still too dazed to do anything but stare. It wrenched Gilbert's heart to see their family in such distress. He spotted Benjie and went to tell him what he'd seen inside the wrecked house.

A man with a notebook questioned the bystanders. "If you saw or heard anything unusual before the explosion, tell me about it." Gilbert recognized him—the detective who had dragged him to jail.

An old man who lived two houses away from the blast had seen something suspicious. "My clock had just chimed two, and I looked out the window. Two tall, shadowy figures raced across my back yard. Moments after they disappeared, I heard a terrific explosion. The ground shook like an earthquake."

Freddie came to join them. "Gunpowder." He wrinkled his nose. "I smelled it."

Gilbert sniffed the air. "I agree. At least a keg of it. Look at the damage to the adjoining house."

"I know the lady who lives in that house—Mrs. Barkeeffer." Vern pointed to the wall next to Corbin House. "Look—her wall looks ready to fall down."

A lady in a bathrobe said, "Windows up and down the block are shattered, even the big plate glass window at the corner."

The captain of the Franklin Fire Guards emerged from the wreckage and reported to the Corbins. "The basement had two spots with smoldering debris. We doused them both." He shook his head. "Look at the destruction—it's hard to believe no one was killed in that explosion. I'd say it's a genuine miracle."

Mrs. Corbin's eyes bulged, and she raised her arm and slashed the air as if she would cut down all her enemies. "I want to get even with the monsters who did this. Corbin House was a showplace for this town, and now it's a heap of ruins."

Gilbert clamped his jaw closed. The ones who did this should be jailed. This evil could not be excused by saying it was for an honorable cause. He had a good idea of the names of the guilty parties. And now he had a strong motivation to bring them to justice.

27
An Unassailable Alibi

Next morning, the Otterbein bells chimed seven times and Gilbert groaned. He'd be late for work again and only get half pay. Or worse, fired. He grabbed a chunk of bread for breakfast and ran out the door. The excitement of the night before would be a prime topic of discussion for the workers. How would Jasper act? Maybe he'd give away his guilt by the comments he made.

Mr. Everal met him and waved away his apologies for being late. "We were wakened by the explosion, too. Had a hard time getting the boys back to sleep." Mr. Everal followed Gilbert into the tile factory. "I want you to unload the kiln for me today since Jasper isn't here."

Gilbert's mouth dropped. "What happened to him?" Visions of Jasper getting injured from setting off gunpowder flashed through his mind.

"Nothing. He and his wife and son left yesterday for a visit to his mother-in-law in southern Ohio."

"Oh." Gilbert's heart sank. That meant Jasper did not set off the gunpowder that destroyed Corbin House. Gilbert could have sworn Jasper and his son had blasted the place.

Mr. Everal chuckled. "Jasper hardly ever smiles, but this trip had him smiling. It's good he could go to their family gathering."

– Choosing Sides –

Family gathering. The words jolted Gilbert like a bucket of cold water splashed in his face. He had completely forgotten the Freeman family event. He half-listened as Mr. Everal explained how to remove and re-stack the tiles. He wrestled again with the question of whether to go home. He'd need to leave tomorrow morning. Yes, he should go, since all his relatives would be there.

"Mr. Everal, I have a family gathering I'd like to miss work for, too. Tomorrow. Will that cause a problem?"

"No." Mr. Everal chuckled. "It will solve a problem, since Jasper won't be making tiles for you to cart away."

Gilbert worked all morning unloading the tiles, a job that took muscle but allowed his mind to examine the evidence against Jasper. Even if Jasper and Lester didn't set off the gunpowder in the Corbin House, did they egg the Corbin Saloon? They must have. He had seen their silhouettes and not many were the size of that father-son pair. Another clue was the small statue of a man he had seen at the Mossman home—it was a dead ringer for the one Mr. Corbin had shown him, the calling card of the vandalizer.

Still, doubt about Jasper's guilt nagged at him. The men who worked at Everal's had talked about a man who'd been seen around Westerville lately. This outsider appeared near Corbin's at odd times, they said. Maybe he was the man he'd seen in the shadows the evening he'd visited Corbin. That was right before the explosion. As an outsider, this fellow might have been hired by someone in town who didn't want to dirty his hands with the crime.

Gilbert liked examining evidence—someday he'd be a real detective. He could start by solving this riddle and earning the reward money. He would need to find evidence against Jasper and his son. They were guilty of at least one of the acts of vandalism, he was sure. Next week after work he would visit Mrs. Mossman and borrow a certain woodcarving. But the Mossmans were out of town today, and he'd be out of town tomorrow.

28
Back to the Farm

After work Gilbert collected his gunny sack from home to hold his groceries. He bought a beef roast for supper and headed to the bakery. The lady behind the counter at the bakery greeted him and asked about his family. "I haven't seen your parents in town lately."

Gilbert winced and gave a vague answer. "Summer is a busy season."

Rose came into the bakery, ignoring Gilbert as if he weren't standing right next to her. She chose several loaves, paid for them, and put them in her basket. Gilbert followed her out the door. "May I carry your basket?"

Rose kept a tight hold on the basket. She lifted her chin and spoke as one would speak to an unfriendly stranger. "I may be weak and easily swayed, but I can carry it myself."

Gilbert followed her as she headed down Main Street toward home. "I said I was sorry, Rose. Will you please forgive me?"

Rose waited until she had reached her porch before she answered. "I might consider it some day, but not today. Good day." She disappeared inside her house.

Gilbert set his jaw and strode home. He guessed it was goodbye, Rose, maybe forever.

~ Choosing Sides ~

As he stuffed things in his gunnysack for his trip home the next day, Gilbert had plenty to think about. What kind of welcome would he get at Freeman Farm? He bit his lip when he thought about Rose. He'd never be welcomed at the Goodspeed house again.

The next morning at breakfast, Gilbert reminded his housemates he wouldn't be there to fix their supper. He chuckled. "In fact, I'm not sure when I'll return. This family event is a mystery."

The walk to Freeman Farm seemed much shorter than his walk to Westerville nearly two months ago. He was eager to see his family, but he braced himself. He knew everyone would tell him why he should stay on the farm.

Near home, his spirit lifted to see the familiar landmarks. Neighbors working in fields and gardens waved as he hiked past. When he saw Old Herman's ramshackle house, Gilbert remembered how he'd been the one who urged him to leave.

He passed two more houses and spotted Pilot frisking near the corner of the Freeman barn. Pilot barked and raced toward him. When they met in the middle of the road, the dog jumped up to greet him and dashed around him in a frenzy of tail-wagging doggie joy.

His grandparents' buggy sat beside the barn. He hurried inside the house. Annie ran to him, her arms outstretched. "Gilbert—you came. I'm so glad you're here."

Gilbert gave her a quick hug. "Did you miss me, Sis?" He gazed at the mirror, the woodstove —everything touched off a memory. "Hi, Aunt Ruby. And Grandpa and Grandma, I haven't seen you in months. How's your garden growing ?"

Grandpa hooked his thumbs in his vest. "We picked our first sweet corn yesterday. We could use rain, and I'm barely keeping ahead of the weeds. We left our neighbor in charge. Didn't want to miss this big family event."

Gilbert listened for hints about why everyone had gathered, but he still had no idea what it could be.

Pa strode over to Gilbert and stretched out his hand. "I'm glad you're home, son. I worried you might not come . . . after what I said."

Gilbert couldn't speak for a few moments. Pa looked so much different—happier. "I'm still part of the family, so I wanted to be here."

Pa glanced at Aunt Ruby and back to Gilbert. "Have you guessed the special event?"

"Not yet." Gilbert noticed the sparkle in his father's eye, the huge smile on his sister's face, and the lace-edged dress his aunt wore. A flower-bedecked hat hung on a peg by the door, and a splendid cake graced the side table. His eyes widened as he added the clues together. "Is it a—wedding?"

Pa grinned like a schoolboy who found a lost coin. "You've guessed it. Would you give me and your Aunt Ruby—your future mother—your blessing?"

Gilbert's jaw dropped. "A new mother?" His eyes swung to Aunt Ruby and stung with tears. She was going to fill that empty spot.

Annie squealed and twirled around her brother. "That's right. Aunt Ruby and Pa are getting married. Aunt Ruby will be our ma." Gilbert brushed a hand across his eyes.

Aunt Ruby came to hug him. "Yes, son. We leave in three hours for church."

Gilbert felt a flood of happiness and his grin almost matched his sister's. "That's wonderful! Pa, you didn't tell me in the letter. What if I hadn't come?"

Annie said, "We wanted to surprise you."

"You did." Gilbert looked around at the familiar faces, and his throat tightened. He'd almost missed this important day.

– Choosing Sides –

Grandpa motioned Gilbert to join him outdoors. Pilot capered beside them and they hiked around fields, past the pond, and through the pine woods of the Freeman farm. Grandpa reminisced about his early years planting crops and raising livestock here.

"Why did you move to Marengo?" Gilbert had been too young back then to understand.

"My father—he'd be your great grandfather—couldn't keep up with the work after the accident that nearly killed him. Your Pa had his family to help him, so I deeded the farm to him and went where I was needed."

Gilbert studied the distant clouds. Grandpa had left his own farm to go where he was needed. Gilbert felt a twinge of guilt, since he had done the opposite.

Grandpa stopped and faced his grandson. "Your pa tells me you plan to go to Otterbein Academy."

"Yes, I've been working in Westerville."

"Doing what?"

"Mr. Everal's Tile Factory—I move tiles on a cart to the drying shed." Gilbert picked up a stone and threw it into the pond.

"You're a hard worker, and that's honest work. But what are your future plans?"

Gilbert found a flat stone and skipped it three times. "This may sound crazy, but I think I'm good at detective work."

"Solved any mysteries yet?" Grandpa gave him a playful jab.

"You're teasing." Gilbert stopped to pat Pilot. "But I am getting close to solving one, maybe."

"You've got farming in your blood, Gilbert." Grandpa had changed to his lecturing tone. "You talk about going to school, but you couldn't have a better teacher than your Pa. He's the best farmer in the whole county."

The lunch bell rang. "Hey, it's time to eat." Gilbert jumped at the chance to change the subject.

"Are you hungry?"

"Yes, sir! Really hungry for home-cooked food," Gilbert said, licking his lips. "I ended up cooking for three fellows to pay my rent. I found out I have a lot to learn about cooking, too."

Grandpa squeezed his arm as they walked toward the house. "You need more meat on your bones. That's a job for Ruby, your future ma."

Gilbert rubbed his stomach. "I'm ready to do my part—I brought my appetite."

Annie ran to meet them as they entered. "Gilbert, sit next to me at lunch. I miss having you to—"

"Boss around?" Gilbert snickered. He didn't mind Annie's motherly advice. He had always teased her about being a bossy little sister, but now he missed their bantering.

She pulled him toward a chair. "Lunch is on the table. Sit here. Uncle John, Aunt Bessie, Uncle Bill, Aunt Libby, and all our cousins will be here soon. Then you won't have time for me."

"I'll always have time for my little sister."

"No, not if you go away again." She leaned toward him and whispered. "I wish you'd stay here forever." Gilbert eyed his sister. She must be part of the conspiracy.

Gilbert piled Ruby's chicken salad high on the homemade bread. He mashed it down to take a bite but had to wait for the lump in his throat to go away. He looked around the table and listened to family news with a new appreciation.

During lunch, Pa had questions for Gilbert. "You said you had a job—who do you work for?"

"I work a half day for Mr. Everal. I move tiles to the drying shed of his tile factory." Gilbert watched Pa's face. "My supervisor thinks I'm not the best worker."

Pa rubbed his chin. "I might have an argument with him."

Gilbert shrugged. "I also worked for Mrs. Everal. I learned some new gardening ideas from her. The Everal boys, Alvin and Frankie, keep me laughing with their antics."

Ruby handed Gilbert the pickles. "Westerville has been in the newspapers lately. What can you tell me about the Whiskey War?"

Before Gilbert could answer, Pa said, "Westerville's battle with Corbin is not black and white. I'm for temperance. But I'm horrified by what some of the temperance forces have done under cover of night."

Gilbert nodded. He and Pa agreed. He was grateful no one commented on how he'd helped the Corbins open their notorious saloon.

Annie was right—the next few hours brought a flood of relatives from out of town.

Uncle John and Aunt Bessie burst through the door. "Hello, everybody! We're here."

Their three boys, younger than Annie, filled the house with happy squeals and shouts. Later, Uncle Bill and Aunt Libby arrived with their five children. Gilbert chuckled as he noticed these five cousins were quieter than John and Bessie's boys.

Annie took her two girl cousins to her room to freshen up. More aunts and uncles and cousins crowded into the kitchen, congratulating the future bride and groom.

Gilbert took Pilot for a walk, figuring he'd thin the crowd. He mused what a big surprise this family event had been. He thought his pa would never get married again. Would he get used to having Aunt Ruby as his mother? It had been good hearing Pa laugh and talk today like he used to do before Ma died.

29
The Freeman Wedding

Gilbert marched into the church among the throng of relatives, neighbors, and friends of both families. Bouquets of flowers lined the front wall and circled the pulpit. The hum of quiet conversations, friends introducing family, and ushers guiding guests to their seats created an atmosphere of anticipation. Gilbert's excitement matched Annie's.

Gilbert and Annie settled into a pew near the front, next to their cousins. They couldn't resist twisting around to see who was in the crowd.

Annie whispered to Gilbert. "The lady with the floppy blue hat in the third pew is Aunt Ruby's neighbor from Mount Vernon. She loaned her a flowery hat to wear for the wedding."

"I've never seen the church this full. There's Old Herman. He never comes, except at Christmas."

The crowd hushed when the pastor, the groom, and the groom's two brothers, Bill and John, dressed in dark suits, stepped to the front.

A bell choir marched forward and, at a cue from the director, played a wedding march.

Annie craned her neck to see better. Two of Ruby's friends, holding bouquets of daisies, promenaded to the front taking steps in time with the music. All heads turned to watch the radiant bride in her pale blue dress, carrying a bouquet of roses and Queen Anne's lace.

Gilbert couldn't help but smile when he saw his father's joyful smile. During the wedding ceremony, Gilbert's heart was tugged in two directions. He needed a mother to care for him, and since he loved his aunt, she would fill the empty spot in his heart. Yet whenever he thought of his own mother, snatched away when her family needed her, he felt a stab of pain. It hurt even more when he remembered his laziness had played a part in her death. He still wondered why God had let that happen.

The pastor's words broke into Gilbert's thoughts. "I now pronounce you man and wife. What therefore God hath joined together, let not man put asunder."

His father turned to the assembled crowd. "Ruby and I invite you to join us at my . . . I mean, our house for a reception. There's plenty of food for all."

Back at the house, Gilbert gaped at the tables loaded with food. Annie pulled him to the side table. "Have you ever seen such a beautiful wedding cake? I baked it, mostly by myself, but Aunt Ru . . . , I mean, Ma helped."

"Is it chocolate? That's my favorite." Gilbert poised his finger above the cake to take a taste, just to see Annie's reaction.

"Don't you dare." Annie swatted his hand away. "The top layer is chocolate. They won't cut the cake till later, so go get sandwiches and salads. And sweet cherries."

Gilbert filled his plate and joined the crowd outdoors. He perched cross-legged in the shade beside three of his younger boy cousins. Gilbert tried to impress them with stories of his housemates' pranks in Westerville. "You should come visit me if you're ever in town."

Old Herman, his plate piled high, joined them. Gilbert watched the tower of sandwiches tilt when Herman slid down the tree trunk and landed with a grunt. After chomping a huge bite, Herman leaned close to Gilbert. "How are you doing in town, sonny? Your Pa never did ask my help after you left."

Gilbert popped a cherry into his mouth. "I'm doing fine, thanks."

The cousins excused themselves and ran to the side of the house. The youngsters counted off fists for a game of hide-and-seek around the horses and buggies parked under the trees. Gilbert wished he could join them, but he didn't want to be rude. He tried to pay attention to Old Herman's complicated story about chasing his cows after they escaped through a hole in the fence.

Gilbert added comments to show he was listening, but parts of the story didn't make sense. Old Herman had probably been drinking before he came.

Herman brought out a flask from his hip pocket. "Here, sonny, this will make your punch taste really good." Gilbert shook his head, so Herman added a generous amount to his own punch.

Gilbert tried to stand, but Herman held his arm. "Don't leave, sonny—I have another story. You need to hear it. If you're going to be a farmer. Ever helped at haying? One time . . . in my younger days . . . I hired out to help, and . . . " Herman retrieved the flask and refilled his empty punch cup. "'Scuse me. I'm feeling a bit dry. It's a hot afternoon."

Gilbert wished he could get more to drink, but not what Herman offered. The rambling story ended only when the flask was empty.

Old Herman reached into his inside pocket. "Would . . . you like a . . . cigar?"

Gilbert shook his head. "No, thanks."

"Nothing like a good cigar after a meal." Herman lit the cigar and blew smoke in Gilbert's direction. When Gilbert coughed, Herman laughed.

– Choosing Sides –

The bell rang, calling everyone inside to watch the bride and groom cut the cake. Gilbert jumped and ran toward the house, glad to be out of Old Herman's clutches. His mouth watered for a piece of the chocolate cake. Guests crowded around the cake table. The groom kissed the bride, and everyone cheered and clapped.

Pa gave a little speech before cutting the cake. "Ruby and I thank all of you, our friends and relatives, for joining us today for our wedding celebration. I took the Bible's advice. It says it's not good for a man to be alone, so I proposed to this lovely lady. With my son Gilbert, and my daughter Annie, we are now a family."

Uncle Bill whistled and a cousin yelled, "Give her another kiss!"

The bride blushed, and the groom gave her a peck, then another for good measure.

Ruby cut the cake and passed out slices to those closest to the table, including Gilbert. When he reached for his cake, she pulled it back. "Is this big enough?" Without waiting for his answer, she handed him one twice as big. "There. You're a young man, so you need a man-sized piece."

Gilbert blushed. "Thanks, Aunt Ruby . . . I mean, Ma. Annie told me the top was chocolate and I . . . thanks."

"I look forward to fixing your favorite things. I can see you're growing fast and need extra helpings to fill you up."

Gilbert tried to think of an answer but couldn't. His new mother was trying to convince him to stay home—that made three people. He edged farther from the crowd around the table and stood by himself in the corner. He gobbled the cake, taking such big bites crumbs fell on the floor. It tasted so good he couldn't slow down. He hoped there would be leftover cake.

He counted all the guests still waiting for their slice. His boy cousins must still be outside. And Old Herman wasn't around for the cake, either. Maybe Gilbert could get another slice soon.

Gilbert glanced at his father, surrounded by friends and relatives. So far, Pa had not been like everyone else, suggesting he stay here on the farm. Maybe now they could talk about his future. Aunt Ruby was a schoolteacher, maybe she could talk sense into Pa about school this fall. Gilbert sighed, remembering the arguments the last two times they tried to talk.

Grandma Freeman hobbled toward Gilbert. "Will you come sit with your old granny?" She nodded toward a pair of chairs nearby.

"Of course. We haven't had a chance to catch up on our news." He offered her his arm, and they settled into their seats.

"Tell me how you're doing these days. I hear you went off to see the wide world."

Gilbert chuckled. "Westerville isn't even as far as Marengo where you and Grandpa live."

"But I've been reading in the newspapers about a big clash there in your little town. Do you know anything about that?"

Gilbert's ears reddened, and he swallowed before answering. "Yes, more than I want to know."

"Anything you'd like to talk about?" She rested a gnarled hand on his arm.

He knew Grandma would understand, so Gilbert began the story at the beginning. "The Corbins, Mr. and Mrs., opened a saloon in Westerville. Vandals in town are fighting them in a shameful way. Like breaking their windows, throwing rotten eggs. The worst things happen at night—like when part of their building was blown up."

"That's shocking. Do you know these Corbins?"

"Yes." Gilbert looked around to see if anyone else was listening in on their conversation. "I worked for them a couple of days, before I knew what they planned to do. They were kind to me. But now I see a different side of them, and I've heard bad things about them . . . ."

"They're not as nice to their enemies as they were to you?"

"Right. I wish I hadn't been part of their plan. I wish I'd never gotten mixed up in the whole ugly mess." Gilbert stared ahead.

"Will you return to Westerville?" Grandma's question made Gilbert squirm. He had been asking himself that question ever since he came home for the wedding.

"I'm no good at making hard decisions. What do you think I should do?"

Grandma squeezed his hand. "You should pray about it. That's the only good way to find the right answer."

Gilbert sighed. "I'm no good at praying, either."

"That may be a signal you don't know the Lord." She gave her grandson a searching look. "God answers the prayers of his own children." Gilbert looked away, but Grandma wasn't finished. "A favorite verse of mine, Proverbs 3:5, tells you how to become God's child. 'Trust in the LORD with all thine heart.' That means to give Jesus control of your whole life."

Gilbert studied his shoes, thinking about his grandma's words. "I need to do that. I've made big mistakes. I'd like God to be in charge."

"You have a Bible, don't you?" Grandma asked.

Gilbert nodded.

"Look up Proverbs 3:6, the next verse after the one that tells you to trust in the Lord with all your heart," Grandma said. "Proverbs 3:6 will help you make decisions. It says, 'In all thy ways acknowledge him, and he shall direct thy paths.'"

Gilbert opened his mouth to answer when three of his cousins dashed into the room, screaming. "The barn's on fire! Smoke's coming out the roof. We saw flames through the window."

Pa raced out the door shouting, "Bill, John, get the buckets from the garden and the back yard. Gilbert, man the pump."

A girl cousin shrieked, and one neighbor woman fainted. Ruby pulled Annie to the kitchen. "Collect as many crocks and jugs as you can. Carry them to the pump."

The crowd circled the pump with the available buckets. Gilbert pumped as fast as he could, and the buckets filled quickly. Everyone formed a line stretching to the barn. Uncle Bill opened the barn door and threw the water on the flames. Inside, the horses whinnied in fear. The noise of them kicking at their stalls made Gilbert shudder.

Pa wrapped a wet shirt around his nose and darted toward the flames. "I'm going in to rescue the horses."

Gilbert's heart beat so fast he could hardly breathe. He worried his father would be injured or killed. He kept pumping, though his arm throbbed, and the blister on his palm bled.

Uncle Bill shouted and stared at the barn door. "Theo's dragging a body out . . . a big man."

Several men from the bucket brigade dashed into the smoke. Coughing, they helped Pa pull the unconscious man into the yard. Pa knelt over him and listened for a heartbeat.

Gilbert stared at the man on the ground—it was Old Herman. They'd talked to each other a short time ago. Gilbert kept staring, unable to move, so Uncle John pushed him out of the way and pumped. The buckets passed from one man to the next. Whenever there was no bucket ready, Ruby thrust a large crock under the stream of water.

Gilbert joined his father, kneeling beside Old Herman. "Is he . . . still alive?" Gilbert stared at Herman's smudged face and closed eyes.

Pa stood and shook his head. "He's gone." He staggered back toward the barn. "The horses—I'm going back in."

Uncle Bill tightened a wet shirt around his nose and mouth. "I'm going, too." He crawled forward on hands and knees, coughing. The flames flickered from the loft, and smoke billowed out the door.

Gilbert ran to join the bucket brigade. "Keep the buckets coming!"

Uncle Bill led out the first horse, a cloth covering its eyes. He guided the frightened animal to safety.

Grandpa, his nose and mouth covered with a wet shirt, disappeared into the barn through the wall of smoke. "Two more horses are in there, and one of them is mine."

Grandma sobbed into her handkerchief. "Lord, help him. And help Theo, too."

The bucket brigade line angled to go around back of the barn. Men climbed a ladder to carry water to the hayloft.

Grandpa burst out of the barn, leading his horse. Grandma waved her hanky, and the crowd cheered.

Ruby peered toward the open barn door. "Where's Theo?" Fear tightened her throat, and her voice became a wail.

Gilbert ran to her side. He squinted into the smoke until his eyes misted with heat and regret. He wiped his face with his shirt sleeve. "Pa's been in there too long." He lunged toward the barn and ducked under the smoke.

Ruby shouted, "Gilbert—No!" She covered her face and began to sob.

Inside the smoke-filled barn, Gilbert crawled toward the sound of a horse whinnying and kicking the stall. The smoke stung his eyes and burned his throat, but he knew he had to find Pa. The fire burned brightly in the stall to his left, but the smoke kept Gilbert from seeing even an inch in front of him. Minutes ticked by.

Disoriented, he turned to the right—the neighing sounds were louder now. Gilbert ran into a hard object—he realized it was his father's boot. "Pa!"

Gilbert felt along Pa's leg and shouted in his face. "We've got to get out of here!" Pa's eyes were closed, and his mouth hung open. He didn't answer. The horse in the stall thrashed to get free.

"Gilbert!" Uncle Bill's shout from the barn door gave Gilbert hope.

"Uncle Bill. Here!" Gilbert coughed, gasping for breath.

Gilbert dragged his father by the feet back in the direction he'd come. Coughing, he felt so weak he had to stop to rest twice. He wondered if Pa was alive.

Uncle Bill shouted, "Gilbert, did you find your Pa?"

"I've got him." Gilbert gasped and tried to catch his breath. "Get the horse."

Uncle Bill crawled past Gilbert and disappeared into the smoke. Gilbert kept dragging Pa until he had reached the door. Uncle John and two neighbors ran to help. They all half-lifted and half-dragged Pa's limp body the rest of the way out of the billowing smoke to the shade of a tree. Uncle Bill dashed out with the horse. Now all the horses were safe.

Ruby raced to her husband's side. "Is he still alive?" She knelt beside him and bowed her head to pray.

Gilbert stared at his father, fearing the worst. Pa's face was black with soot and he didn't move.

Gilbert dropped to his knees and threw his arms around his father "Pa. Don't die. Pa. Forgive me for Ma's death. Pa, don't die. Forgive me for running away. I'll stay. I know you need my help." Sobbing, he repeated the words over and over.

A man with a doctor's bag rested a hand on his shoulder. "Let me see him, son."

Gilbert moved so the doctor could examine Pa. "Is he . . . going to live?"

Annie slipped beside Gilbert, choking back sobs.

The doctor looked down Pa's throat and listened for a heartbeat. He stood and faced them. "He's alive, but barely. The superheated smoke has swollen his airways. His lungs can't get enough oxygen."

Ruby pulled on the doctor's sleeve. "Please, is there anything I can do for him? I'll do whatever I can to help my husband."

"He will need plenty of fresh air and rest. But the damage is done. If he survives, he will always have a scarred throat and weak lungs."

Grandma Freeman put a hand around Ruby's shoulder. "Whether he survives or not, he's in God's hands."

Grandpa Freeman cleared his throat. "Let's pray for him right now." Friends and family bowed their heads in reverent silence. Grandpa Freeman lifted his hands and pleaded with the Lord for the life of his son. "We want Theo to recover, Lord, but your will be done. In Jesus' name, Amen."

Uncle John called to the bucket brigade. "The barn's a goner. No use wearing ourselves out any more." The flames danced through the roof as if they were alive. The crowd stared silently at the fire, many with tears streaming down their faces.

The doctor recruited four young men to carry Pa inside using a blanket. Grandma and Grandpa Freeman, Ruby, Gilbert, and Annie filed into the house behind them with heavy hearts.

The doctor nodded toward the open windows beside the couch where they'd placed Theo. "Close the windows until the smoke from the fire dissipates. When he regains consciousness, give him plenty of water."

Gilbert pulled a chair beside his father. "I want to be the one who sits with him. I have something I have to tell him as soon as he wakes up."

Ruby brushed away tears and put a hand on Gilbert's shoulder. "It may be hours or even days."

"I don't care." Gilbert set his jaw and stared at his father. "God won't let him die. I know it."

The wedding guests came to comfort Ruby and say goodbye. They shook their heads with worry when they caught sight of Theo. Many offered help for any future needs.

Uncle John came inside, sweaty and smudged. "We'll keep dousing hot spots until the fire is finally out." He lowered his voice. "The doctor examined your neighbor and pronounced him dead."

Ruby looked at her husband, motionless on the couch. "Did Herman cause the fire?"

"We don't know for sure." John sighed and turned to go. "I'll stay and make sure the fire's out and come check on things tomorrow. And pray."

Uncle John's last words cut through the fog in Gilbert's mind. He still sat staring at his father, but now he knew what he must do. He needed to pray. Grandma said God answered the prayers of his children. He sat upright when another thought struck him. Maybe he wasn't one of God's children.

Annie slipped into a chair beside her brother. She put her arm around his shoulder. "Gilbert, is Pa going to die?"

Gilbert, lost in his fears, locked his eyes on his father.

Ruby brought a bowl of water, dipped a washcloth in it, and washed her new husband's heat-scorched face. "Theo, this is Ruby. Can you hear me?"

Annie ran to get another cloth. "Let me help, too." They washed Theo's face , arms and hands. The water turned black. His chest barely moved with each shallow breath.

Ruby clasped his hand. "Theo. Your family loves you. Annie is here. And Gilbert is here, too."

Gilbert's lip trembled to see his pa struggling to breathe.

Ruby put her hand on Theo's chest. "At least he's breathing. The Lord is merciful to keep him alive."

Through the window, Gilbert watched the sun set with a fiery glory, a backdrop for the remaining embers of the fire. A lone figure carried a bucket of water and dumped it on a stubborn outbreak of flames. A breeze carried snakes of smoke into the sky.

After many hours of patient watching, Ruby took Annie by the hand. "It's very late. Gilbert, we're going to bed. Call me if Theo wakes up."

Gilbert nodded. He wanted to be alone with Pa and with his thoughts. He looked at the unconscious man before him. He repeated over and over again. "Pa, please don't die."

"Oh, Pa," Gilbert whispered. "I deserted you when you needed me the most." He pounded his fist into his hand.

Squeezing his eyes shut to keep the tears back, Gilbert prayed. "God, you are the only one who can heal Pa. You are in control. Please answer my prayers. Don't let him die."

Outside, a mourning dove called, and its mate answered. Gilbert closed his eyes and grasped his father's hand. "God, I was wrong to run away when Pa needed me. I'll do what Grandma said. I trust you with my whole heart."

Peace wrapped him like a comforting blanket.

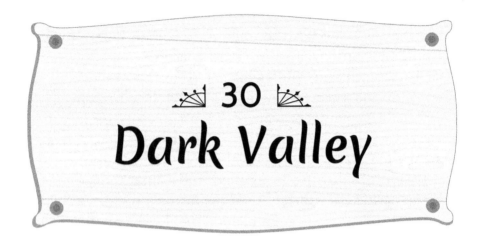

30
Dark Valley

Gilbert, eyes still closed, rubbed his neck where it hurt. Pilot barked outside, and dishes clinked in the kitchen. He opened his eyes—Pa looked about the same. If Pa wasn't getting better, maybe he would die. God wasn't answering his prayer.

Mama Ruby hummed a hymn tune as she stirred the flapjack batter and poured generous circles on the griddle. Gilbert called a greeting to her, hoping she would say Pa was going to be just fine.

She smiled. "Thank you for watching over Theo last night. Did he wake up?"

Gilbert looked back at his father. "No. At least I don't think so. I fell asleep."

"I didn't expect you to stay awake all night. You both needed sleep. His body needs time to recover."

"Will Pa get better? I thought because he was still unconscious, it meant he's dying."

"His condition is serious, but he's a strong man." She flipped each browned cake in turn.

Annie joined them in the kitchen. "How's Pa this morning?"

"Good morning, Annie. Please hand me the platter from the sideboard for the flapjacks. He's improving. Look how much better his color is today."

Annie rushed across the room and peered at her father. "Pa still looks pretty sick to me. When will he wake up? Will the doctor come back? When are Grandma and Grandpa coming?"

"Dear me, Annie. All those questions. Set the table, and we'll talk about it after we eat."

After breakfast, friends and neighbors stopped by, but still Pa had not awakened. Gilbert stayed by Pa's side, waiting and watching.

Uncle John came to make sure the fire was all the way out, then left to buy lumber to be ready for rebuilding. Gilbert stayed beside his father. He wanted to ask forgiveness when he woke up.

In mid-afternoon, Grandpa and Grandma arrived. Grandma set a covered dish beside many others brought by neighbors. Grandma settled beside Gilbert, and they watched the almost imperceptible rise and fall of Pa's chest.

Gilbert asked a question he'd been pondering, "Why did God let this happen to Pa? And the fire, too. Our barn burned down."

Grandma closed her eyes and squeezed his hand. "We can sometimes see the why of things that happen. But when we can't, we know God's purposes are good, even when things look bad."

Gilbert glanced at his new mother, bustling around the kitchen. "I can see one good thing that came from a bad thing."

Grandma followed his glance and smiled. "God uses difficult things to teach us to trust him. We trust him during the unhappy times and thank him the bad wasn't worse." She bowed her head. "Thank you, Lord, for sparing my son's life."

"I'm trusting Him, too, like you said."

Grandma squeezed his hand. "God is giving you a chance to practice your faith in this time of trial."

31
Forgiven

That night, as the clock chimed eight, Pa's eyes fluttered open. Gilbert reached forward and touched his face. "Pa!" His heart was full of all the things he needed to talk about, but he could say only one word.

Ruby brought a glass of water. "Dear Theo. Thank the Lord, you're awake. You must be thirsty."

Gilbert helped his father sit up, then held the glass to his lips. "Sip slowly, Pa."

Annie held Pa's hand. Tears ran down her cheeks, and she whispered, "Pa, you're back with us."

Pa's voice could barely be heard as he croaked, "I'm back here? I was . . . up there before."

Ruby put her arm around his shoulder. "We've been praying for you. The angels were taking care of you."

Pa lay back and closed his eyes. "The angels washed me . . . and held my hand. And prayed over me . . . "

Mama Ruby reached one hand to Gilbert and the other to Annie. "See, the Lord used us to be his helpers." She patted Pa. "Would you like a cup of chicken soup?" When Pa nodded, she hurried to heat it for him.

Annie held Pa's hand. "Uncle John came with a load of lumber. He says the neighbors plan to have a barn-raising maybe next week."

Gilbert tried to encourage Pa. "The horses—all three that were in the barn, got out safely."

Pa reached out to squeeze Gilbert's hand. "How . . . did I? Last I knew . . . smoke, and . . . hearing our horse . . . frantic."

Annie's eyes were bright with unshed tears. "When you didn't come out again, Gilbert crawled through billows of smoke to get you." She put her hands over her face. "I thought both of you were . . . ."

Ruby brought the cup of soup. "But we prayed, and Gilbert dragged you out."

Gilbert's ears reddened. "Let me help you sit up, Pa." When Pa was ready, Gilbert spooned the soup into his mouth.

Pa leaned his head back. "Mmm, good. Soothed my throat."

After Ruby told Pa many more details about the fire, she stood and motioned to Annie. "Tomorrow is the Lord's Day. Come help me iron our clothes—they're so full of wrinkles they're not fit to be seen."

As soon as they were gone, Gilbert took a deep breath and reached for Pa's hand. "Pa, I've had plenty of time to think about things."

Pa put his hand over Gilbert's hand.

Gilbert struggled to find the right words. "I was wrong to run away. I disobeyed you."

Pa squeezed Gilbert's hand. "I'll take part of the blame, too."

"No, I was selfish. I wanted to be on my own. You're my father, and I should've obeyed you."

Pa nodded and closed his eyes. "That's what the Good Book says."

"Can you forgive me?"

Pa put his arm on Gilbert's shoulder. "Of course, I forgive you. You're my son, and I love you." The silence between them lengthened.

Pa turned to face Gilbert. "I need to . . . ask . . . your forgiveness, too."

Gilbert's eyes widened.

Pa studied his son. "I lashed out at you." He took a sip of water. "I spoke harshly—grief makes people do strange things."

"You had a right to blame me . . . ." The lump in Gilbert's throat strangled his next words. "I caused Ma's death."

The clock chimed ten times, each stroke sounding like a death knell to Gilbert. Tears sparkled in Pa's eyes. "Son, did you think I blamed you?" Pa put his face in his hands. "No. I didn't fault you for a moment. What a heavy weight on your heart."

Gilbert shook his head. "But it was my calf . . . ."

"No. It wasn't your fault." He reached to touch Gilbert's hand. "It could have been one of the other calves."

Gilbert looked up at the weathered face of his father. "But, why . . . ?"

"Why your ma died so young, we may never know till we get to glory."

Gilbert blinked back tears as he hugged his father, and his father hugged him back. A feeling of peace filled his heart.

32

Old Herman's Funeral

The day of Herman Smith's funeral promised to be a typical August day in Ohio—hot and humid. Pa sat at the table sipping the honey and vinegar-water she'd made for him. Ruby bustled around the kitchen fixing breakfast. "I suppose you want to attend the funeral today?"

Pa took a sip of the healing potion. "Yep."

Gilbert looked at his pa's bloodshot eyes. "Are you strong enough? It's a long ride to town."

Ruby brought him a bowl of warm oatmeal and a boiled egg. "Try this oatmeal and egg—they will slide down your throat as easy as butter across a warm pancake."

"Thanks, Ruby. I need strength for Herman's funeral."

"I think we should stay home." Ruby put one hand on her hip and shook her head. "It's too hot to go anywhere today. Weather signs say we'll get an afternoon thunderstorm—it might be another gully-washer."

"We need to go to the funeral." Pa's voice sounded weak and raspy. "Herman was our neighbor."

Annie looked up from her breakfast. "I can stay home with you, Pa. Gilbert can take Ma."

"No." Pa struggled with another bite of oatmeal. "I want the whole family there."

Ruby named several more reasons why the family should stay home instead of attending the funeral. She saved the most important one till last. "Theo, you're still weak. You need more time to recover."

Pa set his mouth in a line. "None of your reasons hold water. We're going. Otherwise it looks as if we're holding Herman responsible for the loss of our barn."

Ruby sighed. "At least we can stop at the doctor's in Westerville. He might have medicine for your throat. You can barely speak above a whisper."

Gilbert hitched the horse to the buggy and pulled it around to the front of the house. This would be his first time back to Westerville, and he wondered whether he should contact his housemates. He needed to visit the Everals to tell them why he hadn't come back to work. And he'd like to visit Rose. He hoped she'd be ready to forgive him. As he waited for everyone, he remembered another important visit he might be able to make—an evidence-collecting visit.

Ruby and Annie climbed into the back seat, looking somber. Ruby wore a black dress and Annie's was dark blue. Pa came out last, wheezing and using a cane.

Gilbert hoped this trip wouldn't be too tiring for his pa. He looked pale and hunched over, like a bony, black-suited scarecrow.

Pa climbed beside Gilbert, who offered him the reins. "No, you drive, son. I'd appreciate that."

With the buggy rocking gently from side to side, and the horse's hooves clopping in rhythm, Gilbert gathered courage to start an important conversation. He glanced at his father. "Pa, I found out something about myself while I was in Westerville."

"What's that?"

Gilbert bit his lip. "I like hunting down clues. If I get to go to school . . . ." Gilbert stopped, worried he might start an argument.

- Choosing Sides -

Pa looked across the field. "This year's corn harvest may beat last year's." He looked at his son. "If you went to school, what would you do?"

"If I went to the Otterbein Academy, then someday I could become a detective."

Pa gazed across the fields. "A detective? You've got a keen mind, but have you hunted down any villains?"

"I think I know who's been vandalizing Corbin's Saloon."

Pa stiffened.

Gilbert hurried to say more. "I haven't been buying any of what he's selling, Pa. Don't worry."

"If you help Westerville end the crime spree, we'd be proud of you." Pa turned to watch the crows land in a neighbor's bean field. "But farming—that's a skill you'll need in your future."

Gilbert gripped the reins tighter, as if to hold on to his dream of going to school. He hated to admit it—Pa was probably right. He needed to learn how to farm. "Grandpa tells me you're the best farmer in the county."

Pa chuckled. "No, it's Grandpa who's really the best one."

Gilbert grinned at Pa. "But you're the one I want to teach me everything about farming."

Pa brushed his hand across his eyes. "Hearing you say that is good medicine, son."

Gilbert listened to the even clip-clop of the horse's hooves. He and Pa had talked about his future, and nobody got mad. But Pa hadn't changed his mind. Gilbert needed to look up that verse Grandma said would help him make decisions.

Gilbert pulled the buggy under a tree on the grounds of Otterbein University. He recognized a few of the people entering the United Brethren chapel, the place he'd attended the temperance meetings. He wondered if Old Herman ever visited this church when he was alive. If he'd come to hear the temperance preaching, he might not be there in a coffin.

Once they were inside, they quickly slid into a pew, since Pa couldn't stand long. The solemn mood today contrasted with the buzz of excitement during the temperance meetings. Gilbert scanned the crowd, hoping he'd see the Everals or the Goodspeeds. There in the front row was Herman's wife, two daughters, and son, Stanley, Gilbert's friend. Stanley looked much older since last Gilbert had seen him. It was sad to think Stanley and his sisters lost their father twice.

Mr. Corbin sat by himself in a back pew. Gilbert guessed maybe Old Herman was a regular customer at the saloon. Did everyone at the funeral know the details of Old Herman's death?

Ruby whispered to Pa. "Pretty small crowd."

Pa pulled out a handkerchief and coughed into it. "I'm glad we came."

An older lady with a large hat stood to sing "Abide with Me." Next, a tall, bearded man stood behind the pulpit to preach. Gilbert recognized who it was—Rev. Robertson, the favorite temperance preacher of the Goodspeed girls.

"Friends, we are gathered here to comfort the living after the passing of one from our midst, Herman Smith. Our comfort comes from the Lord, the one who has conquered death. We read in the book of John the words Jesus spoke to the grieving Martha, whose brother had been dead four days. 'I am the resurrection and the life: he that believeth in me, though he were dead, yet shall he live.' Jesus gives us that precious promise, too. Death is our enemy, one each of us must face sooner or later.

"Look around you. You see kind, helpful people, well-dressed, and probably regular church-goers." Gilbert glanced both directions and nodded. He agreed everyone looked pretty respectable.

"Yet even the best man or woman faces the same fate some day in the future—death. Death. Why is death the fate of every one on earth? Because we earn it. The Bible declares this fact clearly in Romans 6:23. 'The wages of sin is death.'

"Perhaps this statement comes like a slap in the face, an insult, to some of you today. You protest you've never murdered anyone. You pay your bills on time, and you help a neighbor in need. You eschew the temptations of the world, like alcohol." Reverend Robertson leaned forward and looked at Pa. "One man here today risked his life to pull his neighbor from a burning barn." Gilbert glanced at his father and saw others looking too. "That was a courageous thing to do, and we all thank him for it.

"Yet none of these good things will help you avoid paying for your sin.

"Friends, do not despair! There is a solution to this dilemma. The same verse that warns us we all deserve death also gives us God's solution. The rest of Romans 6:23 tells us 'the gift of God is eternal life through Jesus Christ our Lord.' Christ takes our punishment and gives us eternal life. What a precious gift, and it is free for every one who believes.

"We never know when our time to die will come. The man who lies in this casket did not plan to leave this life when he did. Perhaps he was prepared, perhaps not—I do not know. Everyone will spend eternity somewhere. Make sure you will be in heaven with the Lord."

Gilbert smiled, remembering how Pa's close call helped him trust the Lord. He glanced at Pa and Mama Ruby—they were smiling, too, but Annie's cheeks glistened with tears. He'd ask her about it later.

The pastor closed his Bible and stepped away from the pulpit to make an announcement. "The Smith family wishes me to convey their thanks for your presence today. Those who wish may attend the graveside service at the cemetery in a half hour."

People stood and greeted each other in quiet tones. Gilbert scanned the crowd for Mr. Corbin but didn't find him. He figured the saloonkeeper must have hurried out the door. Did he feel guilty for Old Herman's death?

Gilbert searched out Stanley Smith, Herman's son. Gilbert didn't know what to say, so at first he shook hands. "I'm sorry about your father. I know what it's like to lose a parent. My mother died eight months ago."

"Then we both know sorrow." Stanley looked beyond the crowd to a place in his memory. "We used to have fun, you and me, when we went fishing, and—"

"Those lazy days when we could do whatever we wanted. I miss those times, too."

"Nothing was the same after my parents split up. We moved to Westerville, and now I'm the man of the house."

"I come to Westerville sometimes. Maybe I'll see you around town."

Gilbert found Pa surrounded by a crowd of men asking to shake his hand. "You're a hero," one man said. "Thank you for trying to rescue my brother," another said.

Pa shook his head. "I didn't know he was in the barn—I went in to save my horses. Of course, a man is more valuable than a horse, so I pulled him out."

Ruby tugged on her husband's arm. "Time to go, Theo. We can't let you get overtired."

Gilbert helped Pa into the buggy. "May I run a few errands while you're at Dr. Coble's? I'd like to stop by the Everals. I feel bad about not giving my quitting notice at work."

Annie brightened. "Can I come, too?"

Gilbert grinned. "Sure. I need a partner."

Annie lifted her chin and clapped a hand to her chest. "I feel honored."

33
Collecting Evidence

Gilbert delivered Pa and Mama Ruby to Dr. Coble's office on South State Street.

Mama Ruby said, "Don't hurry. We may have a long wait to see the doctor since we don't have an appointment."

Annie moved to sit beside her brother. "Will I get to meet those funny boys you told me about?" Gilbert's heart warmed to see a smile on her face again.

"Yes. I'll stop at the Everals first. Frankie and Alvin are their names."

When the buggy arrived at the Everal house, the two boys were chasing each other around the yard. When they saw Gilbert, Frankie and Alvin raced to greet him. "Is she your sister? The one you told us about?"

"Yes, this is Annie. Why don't you give her a tour of the garden and let her meet your dog. I'll go talk to your mother. Is she in the kitchen?" They nodded.

The boys pulled Annie toward the garden and yelled for their dog.

Mrs. Everal's eyes sparkled when she saw Gilbert. "So nice you stopped by." She dried her hands on a towel and waved her visitor to a seat. "We heard about the barn fire. How is your father's recovery going?"

"Pa felt well enough to come to the funeral of our neighbor, Herman Smith. But he will take a while to get his strength back. I'll be needed more than ever to help run our farm. That means I won't be back to work at the tile factory or to help you in the garden."

"You've made the right decision, but we'll miss you." She glanced out the window. "Did my two mischiefs see you when you arrived?"

"Yes, they're showing Annie around right now. Thanks for your kindness, and for giving me a job. Thank Mr. Everal, too. Even though I didn't get to attend Otterbein, I learned a lot from you and from my time at the tile factory."

"Stop by to say hello any time you're in town, you hear?"

Gilbert stood to leave. "Did people say anything about how the barn fire started?" When Mrs. Everal shook her head, Gilbert bit his lip. "There's a good chance Herman Smith started it, since he had been drinking, and he was smoking a cigar right before the fire broke out."

She shook her head. "That makes his death even more tragic."

Gilbert looked off into the distance. "I used to think Westerville was overdoing the temperance thing."

"But since Herman died, you feel differently?"

"I feel the same about all the vandalism and the cruel way they treated the Corbins, but I've seen the terrible effect of alcohol."

Frankie and Alvin burst in the door, laughing, with Annie close behind. "We have a new friend," Alvin said. "Her name is Annie, and she can run really fast."

"Hello, Annie," Mrs. Everal said. "I'm glad I get to meet Gilbert's sister. You're welcome to come visit any time your family comes to town."

Annie and Gilbert said goodbye and climbed into the buggy. Gilbert turned the horses away from town, but Annie didn't notice.

Gilbert glanced at his sister. "It's always sad when somebody dies in an accident, but you didn't know Mr. Smith very well. Why were you crying at the funeral?"

Annie's face crumpled. "I wasn't crying for him. I was thinking about what the preacher said." Her voice quavered. "I'm not ready to die and it scares me."

Gilbert mulled this over. "When Pa almost died, I thought about eternity, too. I needed Pa's forgiveness, and I worried I wouldn't get a chance to ask him."

"I've done things I know are wrong. I felt awful afterward, but. . . . " Annie's voice trailed off.

"But you didn't ask forgiveness?" Gilbert asked. "When I asked Pa to forgive me, I knew I needed to ask God's forgiveness, too."

Annie sighed as she clasped and unclasped her hands. "I don't really know how to pray."

"I had that problem, Grandma helped me."

Annie closed her eyes, thinking. "When Grandma comes to visit again, I want to talk to her about it."

"I wish I knew more about the Bible." Gilbert said. "I'd like to listen in when you have that talk."

Gilbert pulled the horses to a stop in front of the Mossman home.

Annie gaped at the unfamiliar surroundings. "Whose house is this?"

"I'll tell you later. Stay here and I'll be right back."

He knocked on the door, and Mrs. Mossman answered. "Why, Gilbert. What a surprise. Lester isn't here right now, but I'll tell him you came for a visit."

Gilbert cleared his throat. "I'm not here to visit Lester, so that's fine that he's not here. Could I borrow one of Mr. Mossman's carvings? I remember seeing it when I visited you before."

"Come in, won't you?"

"My sister is waiting for me in the buggy. If you don't mind lending me one of the carvings . . . "

She fluttered her hands in the air. "Oh, my, no! This house is so full of them, I'd never miss one if you sneaked in and stole it."

Gilbert's laugh sounded fake, even to him. "Thank you, Mrs. Mossman. I'd only like to borrow it—the carving of a man that's in two pieces. I think it was on a shelf in your dining room?"

"Of course. My husband will be flattered you're interested. Wait here and I'll be right back." In moments she returned with a wooden figure of a man. "I never liked this one, anyway. It's creepy, the way the man comes apart."

"That's the one. Thank you very much. But please don't say anything about it to anyone." Gilbert returned to the buggy, handed Annie the carving, and drove away.

Annie stared at the carving and turned it over in her hand. She took it apart. "What's this for?"

Gilbert gave Annie a long look. "The short version of a long story is that this carving may be evidence against the vandal who has damaged both Corbin buildings."

Annie's eyes were wide. "Are you in danger?"

Gilbert chuckled. "If the person who gave this to me doesn't tell her son or her husband, then I'm safe. It will be our secret."

Gilbert guided the buggy along Main Street, but instead of turning on State to get to Dr. Coble's office, he continued two blocks further. He stopped in front of a two-story brick building and tied up the horse to the hitching post. "Here's where the carving is going."

Annie read the name on the sign. "City council building. Why here?"

"Because we want to help bring justice to Westerville. Carry it for me, will you, Annie?"

Gilbert strode to the front desk and spoke to the same official who jailed him for trespassing. "Sir, I'd like to deposit a piece of evidence against a suspect in the vandalisms of the Corbin Saloon."

The deputy's eyes widened. "Weren't you the one—"

"Yes, I spent a night in your jail, but I was innocent." Gilbert took the figure from Annie. "The man who carved this —Jasper Mossman—he's the one you should investigate."

The man took the statue and studied it. "Yes, it looks just like the ones found after several of the acts of vandalism. Where did you get it?"

"It was loaned to me by Mrs. Mossman, Jasper's wife. Will you return it to her at the end of your investigation?"

"Yes. Let me fill out an evidence card. I'll need your name, address, and signature at the bottom." He bent to write a description, dated the card, and handed it to Gilbert. "We'll follow up on this, for sure."

"I worked with Mr. Mossman at Everal Tile. The other workers can verify that he made verbal threats against the Corbin Saloon." Gilbert filled out the card and handed it back.

The deputy jotted notes on a file card. "I'll give our investigator that information, too. If Mossman is the one, you're in line to get reward money."

Gilbert raised his eyebrows. "Thank you, sir. Let me know your progress."

On the way to Dr. Coble's to pick up Pa and Mama Ruby, Gilbert said to his sister, "We'll keep the last two visits a secret. I may never get any reward money, so we don't want to get their hopes up."

Annie grinned. "It's such an exciting secret, it'll be hard to keep."

34
Famous Detective

Things were almost back to normal at the Freeman Farm. Uncle John and Gilbert, with help from many neighbors, had finished rebuilding the barn. Pa had surprised everyone by regaining enough strength to do light work. Gilbert worked alongside him and found he liked learning from the best farmer in the county. However, he hadn't given up hope that he might still get to go to school.

Mama Ruby and her right-hand helper Annie took care of the chickens and the garden. Annie enjoyed churning the butter and cooked supper on wash day.

Gilbert's thoughts often returned to the evening of the Ice Cream Sociable. It had been four weeks since Rose had slammed the door in his face. He hoped Rose was thinking of him, too.

When he explained the problem to Mama Ruby, she clucked her tongue. "We don't want to let any more time pass before we heal that wound. We'll invite the whole Goodspeed family to Sunday dinner."

Gilbert jumped up. "That's a great idea. Rose won't be able to say no, since we're inviting the whole family."

"I'll post a letter to them today." Mama Ruby walked to her desk and sat down. She dipped her pen into the inkwell and wrote with a flourish.

Gilbert walked to the window, imagining the upcoming visit. "Annie will make a big hit with the girls—Rose and Iva. I'll show them around the farm. And Mrs. Goodspeed will want to see your chickens. She once asked me advice about her flock, but I didn't know the answer."

Ruby selected an envelope. "What street do they live on?"

"Grove Street. And Pa will want to give Mr. Goodspeed a tour of the farm."

While the days dragged by, Gilbert watched the mailbox for a reply. One day he raced inside, waving an envelope. "Open it right away. I can't stand it."

Mama Ruby put down the pastry blender and wiped her hands on a towel. "You're not worried they'll say no, are you?"

"Yes, well, no. I don't know. Just open it, please?"

Ruby read the delicate script. "Dear Freeman Family, We would be delighted to come for Sunday dinner this coming Lord's Day. We'll attend sacred services in town and arrive soon after noon. Please allow us to provide the dessert, a cobbler made with cherries from our own tree. Sincerely, Rose, for all the Goodspeed Family."

Gilbert grinned. "Rose wrote it and she said she'd be delighted to come. Maybe she's not mad at me anymore."

Ruby handed Gilbert the letter and went back to rolling pie dough. "Better wait and see. Be polite and watch her reaction to you."

"Maybe I could give her something, like a peace offering." Gilbert looked around the kitchen and noticed the rack of silver spoons. Some of them had belonged to his mother. An idea sprouted as he remembered sharing a spoon with Rose at the ice cream sociable. "Could I have one of my mother's spoons to give to Rose?"

"A spoon so she can share more ice cream with you?" Ruby's eyes sparkled. "I think that would melt her heart."

Gilbert chose a dainty one and showed it to his new mother. "She'll like this one with a rose on the handle, don't you think?"

"Yes. I'm sure she will." Ruby put the last crimp into the top of her piecrust. "Now please open the oven so I can pop this pie in to bake."

On the Sunday of the Goodspeed visit, Gilbert and Annie helped fix dinner. Gilbert showed off his skill making gravy, and Annie rolled out a batch of biscuits. When the Goodspeed buggy pulled in front of the house, Gilbert's face turned red and his hands got cold. He wondered what he should say to Rose--maybe act as if they'd never had an argument?

Mama Ruby took off her apron and hung it on a hook. "Annie, hang up your apron, too. Gilbert, comb down your cowlick." Ruby rushed back to the kitchen. "Oh—the biscuits!" She grabbed potholders to take the biscuits out of the oven.

Gilbert combed his hair by the front hall mirror as the doorbell rang. He opened it, and there stood the Goodspeed family, dressed in their Sunday best.

Iva carried a covered dish. "Hello, Gilbert. We're here. We brought you a dessert you really like—but don't peek."

Gilbert tried to greet everyone, but when he locked eyes with Rose, he forgot what he was supposed to say. She was even prettier than he remembered.

Annie crowded beside him. "Hello. You must be the Goodspeeds. I'm Annie. Come in and have a seat in the parlor."

Gilbert took Iva's covered dish, glad to have a task. "I'll take this to the kitchen." While he was there, he took a big drink of cold water, hoping to settle his nerves. He forced himself to join the rest of the family in the parlor. When he stepped into the room, conversation stopped.

Mr. Goodspeed strode toward Gilbert, his hand outstretched. "Let me shake hands with Westerville's most famous detective."

Gilbert's confused look made Iva and Rose laugh.

Pa stared at Gilbert, then back to Mr. Goodspeed. "We'd like to hear the whole story."

Mama Ruby sat down beside Annie. "Dinner can wait. This sounds exciting."

Mr. Goodspeed put a hand on Gilbert's shoulder. "This young man gave the tip that led to the arrest of the vandals—the ones who trashed both of Corbin's saloons."

Pa looked at Gilbert and grinned. "You told me, but I guess I didn't believe you."

Gilbert's mouth dropped open. "I gave a tip, but who followed the clues?"

"A private detective hired by the city of Westerville did the legwork—a fellow by the name of McKenzie. He gathered enough evidence so the constable could arrest Mossman."

"Is he fairly tall, and slender? I think he was the one . . . " Gilbert stopped short. Detective McKenzie had arrested him, but he hadn't ever told anyone about his night in jail. "He was the one I saw hanging around Corbin's Saloon one night when I walked past."

"Yes, he worked hard on the case." Mr. Goodspeed took out a newspaper from his jacket. "Let me read this article from the Ohio State Journal. It's dated September 18, 1875.

Headline: Four Charged in Whiskey War Vandalism. Thanks to a tip, the longstanding mystery of the vandalism against Corbin Saloon and Corbin House has been solved. Jasper Mossman, age 41, of Westerville, was arraigned in Columbus yesterday, charged with five counts of destruction of property. His son, Lester Mossman, age 14, will be tried separately before a juvenile court for his part in one act of vandalism against the Corbin Saloon."

Mr. Goodspeed paused and looked up. "Did you know Lester? He's about your age."

Gilbert pressed his lips together, deciding to keep silent about all the bad things he knew about Lester Mossman. "Yes, I know him. That's scary—a boy my age will be on trial."

Mr. Goodspeed continued reading.

"Jasper Mossman hired two accomplices to set the gunpowder charge that severely damaged the Corbin House two weeks ago."

Gilbert rubbed his chin. "Jasper left town the day before Corbin House blew up—just so he'd have a good alibi. Ha! They caught him anyway."

Pa thumped his fist into his palm. "Justice has been served, and I'm glad of it."

Mama Ruby put her hand on her hip. "But is Corbin still running his saloon?"

Mr. Goodspeed beamed, and his side-whiskers moved toward his ears. "Corbin's gone. I walked past Corbin's place on State Street— that eyesore had a For Sale sign out front."

"A group of businessmen want to buy it, to fix it up." Mrs. Goodspeed leaned back with a sigh. "I'm glad—it'll make the uptown beautiful again."

Pa drew his brows together in a frown. "I'm thankful Corbin is gone, but not proud of the explosion that drove him out."

"I agree, Pa." Gilbert said. "But with Corbin gone, that's the end of the Whiskey War."

Mama Ruby's eyes shone. "And to think that you helped solve the mystery."

Gilbert scratched his head. "But how did you find out about my part, Mr. Goodspeed?"

Rose gazed at Gilbert and spoke for the first time. "Papa has an important job on the city council."

Mr. Goodspeed nodded. "Westerville has been accused of encouraging the vandalism, but citizens voluntarily matched the three-hundred-dollar reward authorized by the city council. My role was to collect the reward money." Mr.

Goodspeed pulled an envelope out of his pocket. "I'm also the one who distributes it. Here's a check for six hundred dollars."

Rose and Iva clapped. Mama Ruby and Pa stared at each other, then at Gilbert.

"You're a hero." Annie said.

Gilbert's mouth dropped open. As if he were in a dream, he slowly reached for the envelope with the check.

Mama Ruby looked puzzled. "Gilbert, how did you know who the guilty ones were when no one else did?"

Gilbert's ears reddened. "It would take me too long to tell all my stories." He glanced around the room. "Let's go have dinner—it smells so good everyone must be hungry."

35
Choosing

Mama Ruby directed the guests to their seats for dinner. "Rose, sit here beside me, and Gilbert next to Rose."

Pa beamed from his place at the head of the table. "Let us pray. Thank you, Lord for judging the evildoers in Westerville and for allowing Gilbert to play a part. Thank you for restoring my strength. And thank you for the food you've provided. In Jesus' name, Amen."

Gilbert used his best manners as he passed each serving bowl to Rose. "Would you care for mashed potatoes?" The words didn't convey what he felt inside. He really wanted to ask, Have you forgiven me for arguing over what doesn't matter between us?

Many interesting conversations swirled around Gilbert and Rose. Pa and Mr. Goodspeed discussed economics and the problems that farmers and businessmen faced. Mama Ruby and Mrs. Goodspeed exchanged hints for taking care of their flock of chickens. Annie and Iva whispered, so nobody knew what they were talking about, but judging from the giggles, they enjoyed each other.

What could he say to Rose? He brightened. "How is school going for you so far this year?"

- Choosing Sides -

"The Academy really challenges me to learn." Rose's eyes sparkled. "My favorite class is Literature. We're reading Elizabeth Barrett Browning's poetry."

Gilbert's shoulders drooped. He'd never heard of that author. He tried to think of something cheerful to say instead of, I wish I were in class with you. "Do you like poetry?"

Rose gazed into the distance. "Oh yes. Mrs. Browning's love poems give me chills."

Gilbert wondered what Rose meant. Rather than spout a dumb remark, he turned to watch Mama Ruby serve dessert.

"Is everyone ready for this delicious cherry cobbler?" Mama Ruby served a bowl of cobbler to each guest. "We get to taste Miss Rose's specialty."

Gilbert savored one bite of the cobbler and whispered to Rose. "The best baker in Westerville wins a prize—a tour of Freeman Farm."

After dessert, Mama Ruby shooed the young people outdoors. "We ladies don't mind clearing up after dinner."

Iva and Annie jumped up from the table, giggling and exchanging glances as if they might be planning a trick. They disappeared out the front door.

Gilbert pulled out Rose's chair. "What are those two up to?"

When Gilbert and Rose stepped on the front porch, the younger girls were out of sight.

"Iva!" Rose called for her sister.

Gilbert's hands felt clammy. "They think we'll try to follow them—hunt for them. I've got a better idea." He led Rose to the porch swing.

Rose hesitated. "We don't have a chaperone."

Gilbert waved to his pa and Mr. Goodspeed through the open window. "Our fathers are chatting in the parlor. They'll keep an eye on us. We need to talk, and this is the perfect place."

Rose sat on one end of the swing, and Gilbert sat on the other, making sure to keep the proper distance. They sat in silence for a while, swinging and enjoying the breeze. They watched a robin hop across the yard, stop, and pull out a worm.

Gilbert wondered how to begin the conversation. He wanted to clear up the old argument, not start it again. "Rose, remember the Ice Cream Sociable ?"

Rose's smile faded. "No. I want to forget— everything." She stared at her hands, clasping and unclasping them.

Gilbert studied her face. "Forgive—and forget?" His heart lifted in hope.

"Yes. So much has happened since then." She lifted her eyes to the bright goldenrod blooms edging the lawn. "Let's look ahead, not back."

He reached for her hand. "Yes, let's forget our silly argument—and look to our future."

Her face shining, Rose squeezed his hand. "I'm ready for my grand tour."

Gilbert chuckled to see two girls racing toward the house, followed by Pilot. "There's our chaperones, right on time."

Annie waved her arms. "Come see what happened in the barn." She pulled on Gilbert's arm.

Iva's eyes were large. "We got to watch . . . come and see. Quick." She pulled on Rose's arm and the girls skipped toward the barn. Gilbert went last, suspecting a trick.

Inside the barn, Rose stroked the nose of one of the horses. "What's so exciting? I've seen horses before."

Gilbert admired the timbers of the barn. "It's so new it still smells like fresh-cut pine."

Annie pulled Rose's hand to hurry her. "Come back to the last stall."

Rose knelt by a tiger-striped cat nursing five tiny kittens. "Ooh! Look at them—their eyes are still closed. Aren't they precious?"

Iva lifted an orange and white kitten, which mewed and struggled until she cuddled it. "Do you think Papa would let us have another cat?"

Rose stroked the kitten in her sister's arms. "Who could resist?"

Iva scrunched her face into a frown. "Papa could." She tucked the kitten back with its mother. "Let's go see the rest of the farm."

The four marched toward the pond, with Gilbert in the lead and Pilot bringing up the rear. "Say hello to our ducks," Gilbert said. "Annie named one Jemima, and I named the other Drake. This year they raised a fine hatch of ducklings."

Iva and Rose tried to count the ducks but had a hard time with the moving parade. Iva swiveled so she could announce her total first. "Twelve ducklings in a row."

Past the pond, Gilbert guided them into the pine woods. "Let's take a rest on my thinking log."

Rose perched right next to Gilbert. "It must be nice to have your own thinking log. What have you been thinking about lately?"

He leaned close and whispered. "You." He cleared his throat and spoke to the group. "I've been thinking about two things—Freeman Farm is one. The other is my dream of going to Otterbein Academy so I can be a detective some day."

After a moment of consideration, Annie stood before the group, as if she were a teacher. "Farmers are the ones who feed everyone else. They're much more important than detectives."

Iva stood next to Annie and said, "Detectives have to figure out what the bad people have been doing so they can catch them. We need detectives to keep us safe."

Gilbert slipped his hand over Rose's hand resting on the log. "What do you think, Rose?"

Rose gazed up at the clouds through pine branches loaded with cones. "Kittens being born, ducklings hatching—Freeman Farm is bursting with new life."

Annie's eyes sparkled. "Growing up on a farm means discovering new things every day. Gil, do you remember the time Pilot led us to a newborn fawn?" Pilot lifted his head, wondering why Annie said his name.

Gilbert nodded. "It wasn't even afraid of us."

Annie bent down to watch a horned beetle crawl toward a patch of blackberry canes. "July's the month for blackberries—we picked enough this year to make thirty-three pints of jam."

Gilbert sat up straighter. "But I have to choose one or the other—the Farm or the Academy."

Rose's blue eyes studied him. "That's a really hard choice to make."

Iva tilted her head. "I think you'd have more fun on the farm, studying animals and things like that."

Rose's face lit up. "Couldn't you split your time? Don't farmers take a rest after the harvest?"

Gilbert's eyes widened. "I never thought of that." He would ask Pa if he could attend Otterbein during the winter. Or perhaps even the fall, after the harvest.

Rose swept her arm wide to include the woods and the farm beyond. "If I had to choose one, I'd choose this farm."

Gilbert squeezed Rose's hand, wishing they were alone. Her words sent a thrill down his back. Rose would like to live on this farm—that meant—the idea was almost too wonderful to think about. "Wait till you see the rest of the farm."

Annie grabbed Iva's hand. "We've got apples in the orchard—let's go, Iva." The girls skipped down the path, Pilot loping beside them.

Gilbert watched them go, then turned to Rose. "Here's a promise for our future." He pulled out the silver spoon.

Rose stared at it and blinked back a tear. "Oh, it has a rose—it's lovely." She clasped the spoon with both hands. "Thank you, Gilbert."

The two walked hand in hand toward the orchard.

Author's Note

The archives of the Westerville Library's History Center provided the facts for *Choosing Sides*. The Corbins' battle with Westerville made headlines in national newspapers. Local newspapers followed the story almost daily in 1875 and 1877-1879. The two periods of time have been telescoped in this novel, which covers a period of seven months.

Gilbert and his family and housemates are fictional. However, his employer, John Everal, was one of Westerville's early entrepreneurs, and we meet his wife and their first two children, Alvin and Frankie. The Goodspeeds are also staunch temperance people from Westerville's past with a daughter Emma (now Iva) but Rose is fictional. The Goodspeeds probably did admire Mother Stewart, who had rallies all over Ohio, but there's no record that she had dinner in their home. Reverend Robertson, Bishop Hanby, President Thompson, and Judge Remmy are historical figures whose actions and words follow what has been recorded of them.

The Corbins did have five children, (and a sixth after the period of the story.) I had no record of their grandma, but I gave her a role in their lives. Some of the Corbins' language is quoted directly from newspaper articles.

I've created the characters of Edwards, the liquor-supplier, Martin McKenzie, the detective, and Jasper Mossman, the grumpy carver who worked for Everal, to give body to the story. The carved figures found after the vandalisms are creations of the author, as well.

The arrest of Jasper Mossman brings the plot to a conclusion. We like to see justice done, but in truth, no one was ever charged for any of the vandalism against either of Corbin's buildings. However, a strange story, never validated, surfaced 44 years afterward. "In 1923, an interesting article appeared in the United Brethren newsletter, The Watchword. It revealed that an Otterbein student, distraught over his drunken roommate who had purchased liquor at Corbin's establishment, blew up Corbin's hotel saloon in 1879. Saved from the evils of drink, the once-drunken roommate eventually entered the ministry."

CPSIA information can be obtained
at www.ICGtesting.com
Printed in the USA
LVHW012000260720
661581LV00001B/90

9 780578 615073